The Christmas Toy

A Holiday Reverse Harem Romance

Krista Wolf

The Christmas Toy - Krista Wolf

Copyright © 2019 Krista Wolf

All rights reserved. No part of this publication may be reproduced, distributed, or transmitted in any form without prior consent of the author.

Cover image: Stock footage — story is unrelated to subject/models

KRISTA'S VIP EMAIL LIST:

Join to get free book offers, and learn release dates for the hottest new titles!

Tap here to sign up: http://eepurl.com/dkWHab

~ Other Books by Krista Wolf ~

Quadruple Duty
Quadruple Duty II - All or Nothing
Shared
Snowed In
Unwrapping Holly
Protecting Dallas
The Arrangement
Three Alpha Romeo
What Happens in Vegas
Sharing Hannah
Unconventional
Saving Savannah
The Wager

Chronicles of the Hallowed Order

Book one: Ghosts of Averoigne
Book two: Beyond the Gates of Evermoore

The Christmas Toy - Krista Wolf

Book three: Claimed by the Pack

The Christmas Toy - Krista Wolf

One

ALYSSA

"So we're moving this window," I said, "and upgrading to laminate I-beams here and here, to carry the additional load."

I leaned across his body, pointing down toward the opposite end of the blueprints. It could've been intentional, but my hair spilled over my shoulder to tickle his beautifully-stubbled face.

"Oops," I giggled. "Sorry."

No, scratch that. It was *definitely* intentional.

"Sounds good," Desmond replied in his deep, velvety voice. "I'll make the change order. If I know that supply house, it shouldn't affect the delivery date."

The lead builder leaned back in his chair, folding his hands behind his head to regard me. Desmond's shirt buttons strained against the expanse of his massive chest. His arms flexed tight, looking ready to burst through the fabric themselves.

God...

Every week we had this meeting. If I were lucky, sometimes even twice. Still, I could spend all day in his office and it wouldn't be enough.

He's so perfect.

"Your hair smells amazing, by the way," he added with a smile. "Like a strawberry sundae."

"Raspberries," I corrected him, trying not to blush. "And vanilla. But thanks for noticing."

Our eyes met, and I batted my lashes just enough to be flirtatious. Desmond never even looked away. He was all business, and always confident. But lately...

Lately he'd been holding my gaze longer and longer.

"We uh, also have that conference call on Thursday," I said to him. "The Randall project. Commercial building. They're looking to—"

"I won't be here Thursday."

I blinked. Possibly in disappointment.

"I'm starting my holiday a couple days early," he said. "Flying out for—"

"Stowe!" I snapped my fingers. "That's right. Your annual Christmas vacation with the guys! And also, uh..."

I tried stopping myself, but it was too late. I'd already put my foot in my mouth.

"Emma," Desmond said, his tone going a bit lower. "Yeah, obviously she's not coming this year."

It was the mother of all faux pas. Everyone in the

office knew about the breakup. Just as everyone knew the three officemates who vacationed for Christmas together every year: Mason, Rogan and Desmond. And for the past couple of years, Desmond's girlfriend Emma — who coincidentally, happened to be the boss's daughter — had been tagging along as well.

"Sorry," I said glumly.

Desmond pulled off his reading glasses, instantly going from a sexy Clark Kent to a gorgeous Superman. His expression went soft, and I knew it was for my benefit.

"Don't be," he said, shrugging one massive shoulder. "The thing with Emma... it just wasn't in the cards."

It was their annual tradition; three single guys without any close ties to family, spending Christmas together by traveling to various exotic locales. I knew they'd been to Bermuda, and once even gone to Europe for a week. But lately they'd been heading north, to some ski house Desmond might've inherited in Vermont. No matter where they went, the whole thing sounded magical to me.

"Well it's *her* loss," I said, folding my arms. "That girl's Christmas is going to be boring as hell this year."

Desmond stared back at me, looking rather amused. "You think so, huh?"

"Oh yeah," I nodded. "Staying down here, rather than heading up north where all the real Christmas fun is?" I shook my head. "Damn, it would feel so good to get out of Florida for a while. Actually see some snow again."

"That's right," Desmond smiled. "You're from up north, aren't you?"

"Jersey girl," I said proudly. I smiled back at him. "With New York tastes, of course."

"Christmas must be weird for you around here, then," he said. "Thunderstorms, instead of snow. Shorts and T-shirts, instead of coats and sweaters."

I laughed. "It was an adjustment, yeah."

"Why don't you just fly up then?" he asked. "Visit your folks?"

I tried but failed to suppress a smirk. "My parents couldn't care less about the holidays. They usually spend it jumping from friend's house to friend's house, getting ripped in the process. They don't even set up a tree."

"That's barbaric," spat Desmond.

"Right?"

"Lack of any real family tradition is one of the main reasons the guys and I started celebrating together," he said, thinking back. "Rogan's parents own a travel agency. They send him postcards every Christmas from all over the world. And Mason's family... well..."

He trailed off for a moment, his expression introspective. Eventually he looked back at me again.

"Anyway, we always have fun together," he said. "This year might be a little different without Emma, but... well, we'll make the most of it."

"I'm sure you will," I replied. "And Emma really *is* missing out this year," I added. "A ski-house in Vermont? With three hot guys..."

The words slipped out, but I still didn't regret them.

Rather than look embarrassed, I doubled down by adding a wink.

"I couldn't even imagine how much fun *that* would be."

Desmond shifted forward in his chair, folding his hands across his desk. When he stared back at me again, it was with a strange new look. Almost as if he were seeing me for the first time.

"No," he said with a sideways smile. "No, you really couldn't."

Two

ALYSSA

Green Valley Builders wasn't very green, and it definitely wasn't set in a valley. It took up the top two floors of a grey, four-story office building. Right dead smack in the middle of eternally-flat, central Florida.

Still, as far as places to be employed it was a pretty good work environment. I'd graduated from Penn State. Finished my masters in architectural engineering, before transferring down here to finish out a three-year internship. The company was young and dynamic, and full of energy. *Tons* of work to get done. Lots of different projects, from residential to commercial.

Florida's building boom became a full-fledged job for me, and I got to experience life in the sun. I liked it here. Even as a northern girl, I totally fit in.

Of course, it didn't hurt that there was never a shortage of hot guys running around the office at any given time.

You had the construction crews that stopped by periodically on the way out to jobs, and the foremen who ran them. They were usually well-built and fun to look at. Dressed all the way down for the Florida heat. Even so, I found myself most attracted to my office co-workers. The guys in button-down shirts and sometimes even ties, who had the benefit of air-conditioning. The guys who showed far less skin, but left a little more to my playful imagination.

And I had a *very* playful imagination.

Still, when it came down to which ones were hottest? I liked the big ones. The beefy, muscular guys who took care of their bodies, and in turn, I knew would take care of me. Thick biceps and triceps, lurking just beneath thinly-stretched fabric. Flat stomachs that could hide beautifully rippled abs, accessible easily by two of three shirt buttons.

For this very reason it was always fun to visit Rogan. Especially since I'd seen him buttoning up his shirt one day, fresh from the gym. I'd been blessed with a two-second glimpse of his sculpted stomach, stretched tight beneath a sleeveless T-shirt. He was just out of the shower. Ready to grab his afternoon coffee, and launch into the second half of his day.

I ran that two-second clip through my mind again now, before delivering three quick knocks and entering his office. We didn't usually have much interaction, but lately we'd been put on the same project. A big one, too. One that could, thankfully, last months instead of weeks.

"Hey superstar," he smiled, spinning away from his computer to face me. "To what do I owe this pleasure?"

Rogan was tall and well-built, and more handsome than any guy had any right to be. His goatee matched

Desmond's, only darker. But it was his light brown eyes — the ones that always seemed to melt me right into my shoes — that always had me stuttering like a schoolgirl with a hopeless crush.

"I— I need your John Hancock on a few things," I stammered.

"My John *what?*"

I shook my head at the vagueness of the reference. Or maybe I just wanted to say the word. "Your signature," I smiled. "On these demo permits."

"Ah."

We reached out at the same time, and our hands brushed. Yup, the shivers were still there. It wasn't the first time, either. Wouldn't be the last.

Rogan looked at the folders for a few seconds before raising a quizzical eyebrow. "I signed these, didn't I?"

Shit.

"Did you?" I asked innocently.

Busted.

"Pretty sure I did," he chuckled. Rather than hand them back to me however, he laid them down and signed them again. I'd probably just go with the first copy, to be honest. It was already notarized.

"Maybe you just wanted to see me one last time before the holiday?" he suggested slyly.

My heart started beating a little faster. I decided to go with it. "Actually, yeah."

"Well that makes two of us," he said, "because I wanted to see you too."

Rogan stepped out from behind his desk, his body sliding closer to mine. We'd been this close only once before: in the archive room, three months ago.

"You did?" I asked, trying to keep from sounding nervous.

"Uh huh."

The archive room. Holy shit, we'd almost *kissed*. We'd been trying to squeeze past each other, and somehow we ended up crotch-to-ass. I bumped him, stopped... then *maybe* I'd ground into him. Or he'd ground into me, it was hard to tell.

From there, he'd *definitely* put his hands on my hips. Maybe to help us separate. But also... maybe not. I'd twisted toward him, and eventually we were face to face. Neither of us cared much about moving anymore. Unless you counted the slow pull of inexorable gravity, as our bodies attracted one another and our faces grew closer and closer together...

But then CLICK! The door to the archive room opened, and Jenny walked in. Bubbly. Happy. Waving a cheerful hello, like she didn't just interrupt the most romantic office moment in all of history. With Jenny in the mix there was nothing left to do but smile and turn away, the spell broken.

Shit, I'd been trying to recreate that spell ever since.

"Here," said Rogan. "I got you something."

He handed me a small box, with a red and white ribbon. I pulled it open, to find a beautiful ceramic mug with a cute little Santa on it.

"Oh wow," I giggled. "Thanks."

"Look at the other side."

I turned it over, and saw three checkboxes. One for 'Naughty', one for 'Nice', and one checked off that said 'I Swear, I Tried...'

"It was either that one," said Rogan, "or the mug that said 'This Might Be Vodka'."

I laughed out loud. "On Fridays, that one might've hit a little too close to home."

"Yeah, I figured I'd stay festive."

"You *do* know this means we have to start getting coffee together," I pointed out.

"Of course," he smiled. "Why do you think I bought it?"

If Rogan's caramel eyes were melting me, his smile was doing me in. He was close enough that I could breathe him in now. He smelled like deliciousness, with a hint of cologne.

"Might have to wait until you get back," I lamented. "I can't believe you guys are leaving soon. I'm jealous."

"Yeah, it'll be good to get up there," Rogan agreed. "Mason and I need to help Desmond get over Emma."

I paused, tilting my head. I had to repeat the phrase in my head to make sure I heard it right.

"You mean... she broke up with *him?*"

"Yup."

"Wow!" I practically gasped. "The way the old man's been treating Desmond lately..."

"I know," said Rogan. "Then again, he *is* her father, so he's probably just being protective. Still... sucks for Desmond."

Since the breakup a few months back, it was common knowledge Desmond was on the boss's shit list. Until now, I just figured it was because he'd broken his daughter's heart.

"Sucks for us too, because she stuck us with an extra plane ticket."

Rogan hesitated, and I noticed his eyes crawling my body. He did it blatantly, unapologetically.

"Too bad *you* can't come."

I laughed reflexively before answering. "Yeah, too bad. I'm not a girlfriend, though. Seems like a prerequisite for the invite."

When he said nothing, I nervously added:

"Maybe I should just date one of you until the new year? I'd love to go skiing again."

My sentence hung there semi-awkwardly, in the silence of the architect's office. Slowly, Rogan's mouth curled into a sly smile.

"Which one of us would you date?" he asked.

Not wanting to push my luck, I spun back toward the open doorway. Before stepping out, I raised my new coffee mug in a toast.

"To get knee-deep in some fresh powder again?" I asked playfully. "Who said I'd pick just *one?*"

Three

ALYSSA

As usually happened right before a major holiday, the office thinned out as the week wore on. Tuesday saw far fewer people than Monday. Wednesday, even less.

At least a third of the staff didn't come back from lunch, leaving a skeleton crew to finish out the day. It didn't matter, really. Most of the builders we dealt with were already seeing the same thing. Their crews had all gone home; leaving early to go Christmas shopping, or maybe even to hit the bars. There was very little to be done, and virtually no one around to do it.

That left the office filled with people like me: the single people. Employees without children, or spouses, or much in the way of holiday responsibilities. We wandered like ghosts down the once-busy corridors, enjoying extremely light workloads. Or in my case, pretty much not doing anything but screwing around on my computer all day while watching the time tick by.

By two o'clock I'd decided my last task would be

dropping the latest quotes for materials off at Mason's office. Then, depending on which of my supervisors might still be around, I could sneak out early.

After all, why should the married people get all the holiday perks?

I found Mason exactly where he always was, typing away at one of two different keyboards spread across three monitors. The whole thing made me giggle. He looked like some kind of modern day mad scientist.

"Hey worker bee."

He spoke the words without looking up, and without breaking stride. His fingers still flew over the clacking keys. Without even seeing his screens I knew they were filled with spreadsheets.

"Hello Scrooge McDuck," I replied, plopping into one of his guest chairs.

"Scrooge McDuck?"

"Well it's almost Christmas vacation," I pointed out, "and you're still working as hard as ever."

The man behind the keyboard nodded without stopping. "And how do you know I'm not watching porn?"

"Because I've watched porn lots of times," I said. "And it doesn't require you to type *nearly* that fast."

All of a sudden I had his attention. I could tell because his hands slowed down, and one of his eyebrows went up.

"Lots of times, huh?"

I flushed just a shade redder. "Maybe."

"And what kind of porn are we talking about?" he asked.

Rather than respond, I let out a short, musical laugh. "Wouldn't *you* like to know..."

Mason finished hammering out his latest string of words and integers, then pushed back from his chair. His gorgeous green eyes met mine, as he shot me an inquisitive look.

"So... I hear you're coming with us on our trip?"

I dropped the quotes on his desk in their usual spot. His question — if it even was one — took me a moment to process.

"And who told you that?"

"Rogan," he replied flatly. "He said you didn't have any plans. That your parents..." he looked up at the ceiling for a moment, "how did he put it... *sucked* at Christmas?"

I shook my head in obvious disappointment. Sucked was putting it mildly. My parents hadn't celebrated anything resembling a holiday in quite a few years now. They just always did their own thing.

"What else did Rogan say?"

Mason sat up a little straighter and moved to smooth out his tie... only his tie was long gone. He'd taken it off hours ago, apparently. I could tell he wasn't used to not having one.

"Well, he said you didn't have any plans for the holiday," he answered. "He also said you knew how to ski, and you might ride our extra ticket."

I tried hard to keep the surprise from my expression.

"Oh *really?*"

"Yes really," said Mason, as he added a half-smile. "And I have to say, I'm pretty psyched. We've discussed it amongst ourselves, and we think you're gonna fit right in."

"*Discussed* it?" Now I really was incredulous.

"You'd better get home and pack," said Mason, looking down at his watch. "And if you leave me your driver's license, I'll transfer the ticket over so—"

"I can't come with you to Vermont!" I blurted suddenly.

"No? And why not?"

"Well for one, I didn't take off."

"So?" he shrugged. "Take off. It's only one more day."

"Besides, this is a guys' trip," I told him. "I'd be a fourth wheel."

Mason shrugged and smiled. "Four wheels is good, no?"

"I mean fifth wheel," I corrected myself quickly. "Or rather... shit. I don't even know what I mean."

"Emma came with us," he pointed out. "She was a good wheel."

"Yes, but Emma was Desmond's *girlfriend,*" I pointed out.

"So?"

"So that's different."

"Not for us," Mason shot back.

I paused for a second to regard him, wondering how much of this conversation were actually genuine. Did he really talk to the others? And if so...

"Emma was Emma," I said finally. "But I'd just be that overly-annoying office girl who tagged along and messed up your guys' trip."

Mason didn't answer, but I noticed he was looking over my shoulder. When he spoke next, it wasn't directed at me.

"See? I told you she wouldn't come."

I whirled in my seat and saw Rogan, leaning against the doorway. Behind him, with his arms folded, stood Desmond.

"You really don't want to go?" Desmond asked.

I was on the spot, now. Totally at a loss. I could've said anything, made up any excuse. Instead, I answered his question with another question.

"Do you really *want* me to?"

Both guys nodded definitively. Seeing them together made me nervous and queasy... and yet excited, all at the same time.

"Skiing," I said. "In the mountains of Vermont. For Christmas break."

"Yes, yes and yes," said Rogan.

"You know," teased Mason, "if you're really *into* that sort of thing..."

"Of course I'm into it!" I breathed. "Who wouldn't be?"

"Unless I'm mistaken," said Rogan. "I'm pretty sure you used the words 'would love to go'."

The guys fell silent as I swallowed hard. I couldn't believe they were serious.

"And it's free?" I asked skeptically. "I mean, I could probably kick in *something* toward—"

"We're staying at my place," said Desmond, "and there's plenty of room. Plus, your ticket's already paid for." He shrugged. "Just say the word and we'll put your name on it."

My mind spun in circles, trying to find any reason whatsoever to tell them no. I couldn't think of a single thing.

You don't really want to spend another Christmas alone, do you?

No, I didn't. And that cinched it.

"Okay."

I saw their eyes light up. Three very distinct smiles warmed their faces.

"Really?"

"Yeah, sure." I smiled back at them. "Why not? It all sounds so amazing, actually."

I watched as their gazes flitted to each other for a moment. Desmond looked at Rogan, who looked at Mason. Some kind of silent understanding passed between them before Desmond turned his attention back to me.

"Looks like you're missing that meeting tomorrow too," he winked.

The Christmas Toy - Krista Wolf

Four

ALYSSA

The next day was a whirlwind, of emotion and travel. There was a knot of excitement in the pit of my stomach as I went home and packed. A schoolgirl excitement mixed with the thrill of the unknown, as I prepared to take a vacation with three beautiful men who were practically strangers to me.

And yet at the same time, they weren't. I'd befriended them all. I'd worked alongside them and spent time with them. Hell, I'd even sort of hooked up with one. All of them had flirted with me in the past. And of course, me with them.

I thought about these things as I stuffed my suitcase full. There probably weren't many Floridian women with a snowbunny wardrobe like mine. Then again, I'd spent most of my life up north. I'd brought back my cutest sweaters and coats and cold-weather outfits, hoping I'd be spending more time visiting friends back in Jersey, or even my family.

But that just never really happened.

I was totally okay with not spending Christmas with

my family. My brother was in the Navy, stationed somewhere overseas, and would send me a card once he reached whichever exotic port he hit next. My sister Kate had embraced West Coast life to the point where we no longer actually heard from her. Any conversations had to be initiated from our end, and she always seemed indifferent to say the least.

That left my parents, who were as disinterested in the holidays as they were in coming down to visit me. In all the years I'd been down here, they'd never once come to my place. Which was a little hurtful, considering they visited their friends in New Port Richey without even asking if I wanted to meet up.

Ouch.

By the time the car service showed up, I was over it though. I'd shoved all those thoughts aside, to make room for the butterflies and excitement I felt when Rogan knocked on my door. He and Desmond carried my things to the driver, while Mason ushered me into the big, beautiful sedan. Then we were off. Holiday vacation had officially started.

Just the thought had me sighing happily.

We had a short ride to the airport, but it was a fun and comfortable one — especially nestled into the soft leather alongside a couple of really cute men. Someone pulled the cork from a bottle of champagne, and the four of us had a glass before reaching the departure gate. I must've asked a thousand questions; what Stowe was like, what kind of cabin we had, what else there might be to do in town. It was Christmas, after all. I wanted to embrace at least *some* of the holiday.

And shit, with some cold and snow? It would actually

seem like Christmas again. Not the watered down, sun-filled, Florida version of Christmas I'd spent the last few years enjoying. But the white-blanketed, teeth-chattering, icicle-covered variety I'd grown to know and love.

As we boarded and settled in, I came to realize my fears of being a fifth wheel were probably unjustified. The guys were fun, and funny, and seemed happy to have me. They joked amongst themselves, without holding anything back simply because I was there. At times I even joined in, laughing and poking fun and even taking a few shots as well. And yes, this is what I wanted. I wanted to be a *part* of their fun and camaraderie, not just some outsider enjoying their trip with them.

We took off, and silently I wondered what would happen during the course of the trip. Whether or not one of the guys and I would make some sort of connection... or if the vacation would be strictly skiing and snowboarding and other platonic fun.

I had a definite connection with Rogan, and if not for the interruption in the archive room I think we both would've already explored it. As for Mason...

Well, Mason and I had already kissed.

It had happened last summer, during the company's annual picnic. Mason and I got drunk together, or at least pleasantly buzzed. We'd been paired up during the three-legged race, and the closeness and intimacy extended afterward, when he took me by the hand and led me to a wooded area of the beautiful park. Then we'd kissed... and kissed... and pretty much made out like teenagers for a good five or ten minutes, leaning up against some big old pine tree in the middle of nowhere.

The whole thing was a blur, but that blur had been pure heaven. The sweet taste of his mouth. His hot tongue, swirling against mine. I remember holding his face, and feeling that sexy stubble beneath my palms as our breathing grew rapid and our hands grew bold. And then we were touching each other. Our fingers roaming each other's summer bodies, in the cool shade of that beautiful clearing...

That's when the whistle blew, signaling the next event. Someone came looking for us, and the next thing we knew we were doing potato sack races and exchanging sly glances and trying not to turn fifty shades of red in front of the rest of our colleagues.

Until that moment I'd always known Mason as prim and proper. Totally by the numbers. Sure, his button-down shirt and tie covered a hard, gorgeous body, but in the office he was all business, all finance.

I never mentioned our little hookup again. In turn, he never mentioned it either. Since we were both pretty buzzed, there were times I wondered if he even remembered it at all.

Finally there was Desmond, who I had *definite* chemistry with. Desmond was big and beautiful and right up my alley. Our flirting had progressed nicely, to the point where I expected one of us to eventually make a move. He'd certainly been broken up with Emma long enough now. And since she no longer worked at the company...

My musings were broken up by the announcement we'd be landing soon. I decided right there to just go with the flow. To not pick any particular guy to go after, but to let one of *them* make the first move if they so desired.

And if they didn't want anything more than a ski-partner? A fifth wheel, to have some fun with? That was okay too. I wasn't out to interfere with the annual holiday trip of three lifelong friends. Or especially, get between them.

Not unless they *wanted* me between them, I joked inwardly, as we deplaned.

Five

DESMOND

The truck was at the back end of Burlington International's maintenance lot, just as Jay said it would be. The keys were already in it. As a baggage handler, they let our friend keep it there while he wintered down south, in return for using the snowplow mounted on the front.

For the whole time we were here though, the big old truck was ours.

The heat only worked intermittently, causing us to huddle together as we drove the hour or so to Stowe. Mason sat in the back seat, jammed up against all our luggage. That left me and Rogan up front... with Alyssa nestled comfortably between us as the vehicle rolled slowly through the driving snow.

She looked amazing, even all wrapped up and dressed for winter. She smelled even better. Like watermelon and honey and vanilla body spray, or whatever the hell she was using to drive us crazy.

And believe me, she *was* driving us crazy. In all the best ways.

It was no secret that I wanted her. Alyssa was that rare combination of fun and gorgeous — a genuinely happy person with a bright, pretty smile. Every time she came into my office I looked for ways to keep her there longer.

But Rogan wanted her too. Something about a missed connection they'd had together. And Mason... well, he'd already sort of *had* her, in a cute, semi-innocent way. Apparently he'd been lucky enough to make out with her at the company picnic, after they'd shared a few beers in the sun together. He was terrified of making any new moves though. Since she'd never said anything afterward, he figured she either didn't remember it, or was simply too embarrassed to acknowledge what had happened.

That left us all in a bind, especially since we had the same thoughts and feelings. So rather than fight for her affections and possibly overwhelm her, we came up with a plan that took care of everything all at once:

We'd leave her alone.

It was a gentleman's agreement; that not one of us would pursue her during the entire trip. That we'd try to have fun as four coworkers enjoying Christmas together, without the added pressure of a budding romance, or the potential jealousy from those of us who'd lose out in such a situation.

Yeah, so... flirting was fine. Anything else? Well, that was off limits. Or at least that's what we *told* each other, anyway. I just wondered how long our agreement would hold out, and how far I could stretch the flirting thing without technically breaking the rules.

In the end though, we hadn't asked her along for any reason other than Alyssa was fun. And while the three of us had never had a shortage on fun on this trip, we knew she'd bring an extra level of happiness and excitement.

Besides, she said she could ski. And keep up. And maybe even beat us.

We'd have to see about that one.

But inwardly, I also knew Alyssa would help with another thing. One the guys couldn't really help with, and one I needed more than anything else this holiday.

I needed to keep my mind off of Emma.

It sucked to admit it, but I had to face the realization that this trip had always sorta been about *her*. From the moment she began coming with us, Emma had fallen in with the three of us in ways that no other person ever could. As my girlfriend, I'd been afraid she'd detract from the normal amount of camaraderie and attention I paid to the guys. Instead, it had been just the opposite. Emma had become the focal point of the trip. Not only for me, but for Rogan and Mason as well.

In three years, this would be our first Christmas without her. Our first Christmas without the things she brought on the trip, too.

Eventually we reached the driveway, and I pushed all thoughts of Emma from my mind. I fumbled with the lever that lowered the plow, and slowly cleared at least two feet of snow from the long trail of snake-like pavement that I had pretty much memorized.

The cabin came into view, all dark and beautiful, its

ice-covered roof sparkling beautifully in the moonlight. Soon we'd light it warmly from within. Mason would gather wood from the pile and start up a roaring fire, while Rogan and I swept the snow from beneath the eaves.

There was a hell of a lot to be done, but I had the guys with me. Together we always worked as a team.

And Alyssa, I somehow knew, would fit *right* in.

Six

ALYSSA

"Welcome home!"

Desmond's voice boomed through the beautiful wood-crafted cabin, carrying through the open expanse of darkness and up into the rafters of the high vaulted ceiling. The place was absolutely amazing. Quaint, yet spacious. Charmingly old, but equipped with present-day amenities like its modern kitchen and flat-screen TV.

The lighting was sparse. I could tell more than a few light bulbs were out. And the place was freezing cold, because whenever we exhaled we all had dragon breath.

But it was exciting. A place like this... it just felt *warm*, even when it wasn't. And the guys would make it good for us. I knew that already. They'd promised to make me warm and cozy and have me 'stripping off clothes' just to keep from sweating, *that's* how hot Mason liked to keep the fire going. And according to the others, he was sort of good at it.

As for me, I just wanted to help. To kick in wherever I

could, and to make the place a home for us for the next week and a half. Skiing at Vale, plus whatever else we did — that was all just a bonus. For me the real prize was getting to hang out with the guys for the holidays, and not having to spend another Christmas alone.

Mason and Rogan disappeared in opposite directions; something about the water heater and getting the plumbing going again. Desmond took me by the arm and led me proudly room by room, giving me the grand tour.

"So this is the family cabin, eh?" I asked, taking it all in

"Well it's all mine now," said Desmond. "When my parents retired to Texas, they told me they were 'finished with the cold for good'."

"Ah, Texas," I acknowledged. "Good choice."

"If you don't like the cold, it sure is."

"So no siblings?" I asked, though I thought I knew the answer.

"No. Just me." He paused mid-stride and shrugged. "Rogan and Mason are like my brothers, though. I guess I'm closer to them than most people I know are with their blood relatives."

I nodded in complete understanding. In a way, I was a part of that sad family dynamic. I had two parents who at this point in their lives were wholly disinterested in their own children. As well as brother and sister who could take me or leave me.

"Anyway, this is the kitchen. The living room. The bathroom..."

He led me down a wood-paneled hallway, complete with creaky floorboards.

"My room's here," he pointed left. "Mason and Rogan are in here..."

We reached the end, and he tried pushing the door open. It bowed, but didn't budge.

"Frozen shut?" I chuckled.

"Yeah," he smiled apologetically. "It happens."

He turned sideways and threw his shoulder forward, breaking the seal. The door opened into a beautiful master bedroom, complete with a king-sized bed.

"This is you," he said, waving one arm grandly. "Linens are in the closet. The down comforters are really warm, especially—"

"Wait, why is this *my* room?"

"What do you mean?"

"It's huge! I'm small. Give me one of the smaller rooms."

Desmond shook his head. "This one has a master bath. You'll need that. You're a girl."

I laughed out loud. "You think?"

His eyes darted over me real quick. "I'm pretty sure, yeah."

"But this is *your* room, isn't it?"

Desmond shrugged. "Usually, yes."

"So I'm not taking *your* room," I objected. "No way!

No reason I should—"

"Look," said Desmond, jumping in. "When I was with Emma, it made sense for us to have the master. We were a couple. She was a girl." He pointed at the attached bathroom. "She did girl things in there. Believe me, I get it."

I paused for a moment, realizing how sweet he was trying to be. Then his hand touched my shoulder, and my eyes found his.

"I'm a guy," Desmond smiled. "In case you haven't noticed."

"Oh, I've *noticed*," I giggled.

"I can sleep anywhere," he said. "It's no big deal. Plus, it's a lot easier for me to share a bathroom with those other two animals." His smile broadened, and I found myself melting right there on the spot. "Please, Alyssa. Take the master."

His hand was still on my shoulder. The tingles radiating from his palm felt warm and wonderful, even through my jacket.

"O–Okay."

Our bodies were close now. Our hips, almost touching. And the way he said my name...

A crazy thought crossed my mind, creating an instant fantasy. In it, I would lean in and kiss him. Our kiss would be slow, sensual. Thunderous. Our tongues would dance while our hands roamed, and then I'd step back from Desmond's embrace and smile coyly and tell him to take the bedroom *with* me.

The moment passed. The opportunity, missed.

"C'mon," said Desmond, pulling me back into the hallway. "You can help me stock the fridge."

Seven

ALYSSA

It took almost two hours to get everything straight. We were unpacked and settled into our rooms. Stocked — at least partially — with whatever drinks and snacks the guys had packed in a separate suitcase.

"You good?"

I smiled, raising my wine in Rogan's direction. I was halfway through my third glass. Feeling absolutely no pain.

"Oh I'm better than good," I smiled. "Fantastic, actually."

"Alrighty then," he nodded, adding a wink. "As our official holiday guest this year, your needs come first."

The cabin was warm now, even cozy. As promised, Mason had the grandfather of all fires going. It radiated outward from the stone hearth, filling the living area with a soothing, welcoming heat.

I was on the strange old couch, curled up against one

of the arms. Desmond sat beside me. Rogan lounged out in an overstuffed lazy chair, while Mason was laying across some leather sofa so old, so worn, it was more cracks and crevasses than actual leather at this point.

"So what's it like?" I asked, staring into the fire.

"What?"

"Stowe. I've never been."

"Well it's a lot like Killington," answered Desmond. "Big and beautiful, with lots of trails. A little more confusing though. And a hundred feet extra of elevation."

I tipped my glass back woozily. "Sounds like fun."

"Oh it's fun," confirmed Rogan. "The question is... which one of us is gonna have to babysit you tomorrow?"

I laughed so hard, I almost spit the wine back into my glass. He was needling me, I knew. They'd all been doing it, ever since I'd boasted I could ski. But babysitting...

"And how exactly are you going to babysit me," I teased, "if you can't even catch me in the first place?"

A round of 'oohhs' went up at the audaciousness of my challenge. Desmond laughed from alongside me. Rogan sat up straighter in his chair.

"Catch you?"

"That's what I said," I replied boldly. "I was thinking *maybe* one or two of you could keep up. Or get close for a little while, anyway. But the way you're all bragging..." I let out a little laugh of my own. "I can see now it's nothing but talk."

Mason got up poked at one of the logs in the fire.

When he turned around again, his green eyes glimmered with the dancing flames.

"You're really talking a lot of smack, aren't you?" he grinned.

I shrugged playfully and drained the rest of my glass. "We'll know after the first run, won't we?"

Another round of laughter from the guys had me turning a slightly deeper shade of red. Mason was right: I was talking a hell of a lot of smack. I'd better be able to back it up.

Desmond held the bottle my way, but I waved him off.

"You're trying to give me a hangover," I said accusingly. "Slow me down tomorrow."

"Maybe."

"Not gonna work. I'm done for the night."

I pushed my glass forward across the pockmarked surface of the room's beat-up coffee table. Not a single piece of furniture in the living area matched any of the others. For some reason, it only added to the charm.

"This place is amazing by the way," I said, changing the subject. "And... I really wanted to thank you guys for inviting me. Seriously."

The room grew silent, except for the snap and crackle of the fire. All eyes were on me, now.

"I need you to know I appreciate it," I finished. "And I'm looking forward to Christmas together."

The wind picked up, rattling the cabin's thin-paned windows. It made me shiver involuntarily, even though I was toasty warm.

"We're thrilled to have you," said Desmond with a smile. "You're our number one girl at the office, you know. For all of us. As fun as you are there, we knew we'd love having you here even more."

He rose and stretched mightily, looking a bit like the Hulk tearing his way out of his shirt. The wine had lowered my inhibitions to where I couldn't stop staring at his chest.

"If we want to be there when the mountain opens, we should probably all turn in," Desmond said. "It's been a long day."

A little begrudgingly the others nodded their agreement, especially since I was leaving as well. Mason stoked the fire again. This time he added enough logs to get us through the night.

"Might wanna leave your bedroom door open," he said over his shoulder. "Or you'll probably freeze."

"Oh. Okay."

I shuffled toward the hallway, bidding them all a good night. Desmond ducked through his doorway, leaving Rogan and I all alone.

"Walk you to your room?"

My room was literally ten feet away. I nodded anyway.

A dozen steps later I was standing in my room, with Rogan following me in. With a deft swing of one hand, he pulled the door almost all the way closed behind him.

Almost immediately, my pulse began to race.

"I wanted to say thanks for coming with us," he murmured. "I thought this year might be a little weird for

Desmond. But with you here... not so much."

We were standing close, almost embracing. Probably so we could hear each other, because we were talking so low.

"Why?" I finally asked. "Wouldn't having a girl on the trip just remind him of Emma?"

"I think it's more of a distraction, actually."

"Oh."

Rogan shifted from one foot to the other. The movement may or may not have been intentional, but it brought us just a tiny bit closer together.

"You gonna be okay in here?"

He nodded left, toward my big old bed. The moonlight spilling in through the window made it look unnaturally cold.

"I think so."

"There's more in the way of blankets in my room," he said, "up in the closet. You know, in case you get cold."

I arched an eyebrow. "Is that an invite?"

Rogan bent down a little more, bringing himself to my level. We were face to face, nose to nose. His goatee was just centimeters from tickling my chin.

"Could be," he breathed, and his breath was sweet. "If you don't mind sharing a bed with Mason's snoring, that is."

The room was considerably colder this far from the living room. Even so, my body felt like it was on fire.

"Maybe you could just come in here?" I teased, though I wasn't exactly teasing. "We could spoon for warmth."

He shifted again, and this time his goatee *did* tickle me. Right on the lips.

"I mean, it wouldn't be the first time we were crotch-to-ass."

Holy shit, I thought to myself frantically. *What the fuck are you doing?*

Immediately I could see the wheels turning in Rogan's mind, remembering our encounter in the archive room. How it must've felt to be pressed up against me. Our bodies so tight in the small, cramped space.

"Who gets to be the big spoon?" he eventually asked.

"Does it matter?"

I conjured up the memory myself, as I had numerous times before. The wonderful hardness of his body. The thick swell of his bulge, moving against my devilish grind...

"I guess not," he whispered.

Our noses touched. Then our lips. It was a slow, inexorable coming together. An electric attraction, just as it had been the first time, when we–

"Well come get me if you need anything."

He said the words with an air of disappointment and underlying frustration. Then, just as quickly as the whole thing had started, Rogan pulled open the door and vanished back into the hallway.

What in the–

Leaving me breathless and alone.

Eight

ALYSSA

I'd been right. The moonlight *was* cold. But the world under my blankets and comforters was warm and cozy, and much softer than I imagined it would be in the big, wide bed.

Even so, I couldn't sleep.

For one, I was excited about tomorrow. From the moment we'd deplaned and the first blast of arctic air had filled my lungs, I'd been totally in love with the cold weather again. I couldn't wait to be on top of the mountain, looking down. Pulling my goggles over my eyes and setting my sights on the distant bottom.

But more than that, I was still confused about my encounter with Rogan.

We'd just kissed... or at least I *thought* we did. And yet the moment his lips touched mine he'd pulled back and bolted from the room without a second thought.

Maybe you misread him?

No, that wasn't it. The chemistry between us was undeniable. From the archive room to our encounter from only an hour ago, there was an undeniable attraction between the two of us. The only difference was that I was willing to act on it.

And for some reason, Rogan wasn't.

The rejection bothered me, and not just for the standard reasons. The whole thing just seemed too sudden. Like he'd been yanked from the room by the slam of a distant door, or the sound of parents coming home when they weren't supposed to.

I sat up and bunched the sheets up around me. I desperately needed to sleep, but I also needed a distraction. Something to make me tired. Something—

On a whim, I opened the drawer to the nightstand. I saw a pair of comfy-looking socks. A tube of Chapstick, strawberry-flavored. Three loose mint candies — individually wrapped. A black Scunchie headband...

Emma's things.

I slid the drawer closed, feeling abruptly guilty. Then, after ten long seconds of feeling foolish, I rolled it open again.

There was a book at the bottom, staring back at me.

No, not a book. A notebook.

Carefully, trying not to make any noise, I pulled it out. It wasn't a spiral notebook, it was more like one of those marbled composition books. The ones still bound with string in the middle.

I grabbed my phone, and thumbed on the flashlight.

Then, settling back against the pillow, I opened the cover and began to read.

Almost immediately I placed my hand over my mouth.

This wasn't just Emma's notebook, it was her *journal*. And from what I could see there were dozens of pages of entries, each one marked and dated.

Holy shit.

I flipped back to the first one. It was penned exactly three years ago, almost to the very day.

Our Christmas Vacation - Day One

The guilt crept back, as I scanned the neat, feminine handwriting. I shouldn't be reading this. It was an invasion of privacy.

She's gone, though.

That much was true, of course. And Emma had broken up with Desmond, not the other way around. She'd been the one to hurt *his* feelings. One of the very awesome guys responsible for bringing me on this great trip in the first place.

Yeah, seriously. To hell with Emma.

With all that finally decided, I opened and began reading again.

The first few paragraphs detailed their trip, which was similar to mine. Their flight was bumpy. They experienced delays at the airport. Eventually they reached the cabin and all kicked back to relax, only Emma and Desmond outlasted the others, who turned in a little early.

That's where things got good. Or rather, they got juicy.

He took me on the couch first, where he'd been teasing me all night. Fingering me under the blanket, with the others just a few feet away. The whole thing was driving me crazy. Making me dripping wet, and not one of them was the wiser.

I continued reading, devouring Emma's first-hand account like a cheap romance novel. Only these were real life events. They'd happened right here — right on the very couch I'd sat on half the night — and that made it all the hotter.

The couch was too small, and way too noisy for us. That's when he took me on the floor. He spread me out in front of the fire, teasing me top to bottom with that big, thick shaft. Pushing my legs apart while kissing me into oblivion. Making me wait forever in anticipation of that first, incredible thrust...

Holy shit! It was getting hotter under the blankets. My heartbeat hadn't slowed at all, but had actually picked up speed since I'd begun reading.

He fucked me slowly at first, like he always did. Kissing me deeply. Getting me used to him again, after our time apart. I laid back and let him stretch me to that wonderful place between pleasure and pain. And then I felt him push past *that point, to reach that tingly spot deep in my belly…*

My breathing was growing rapid now. It felt like I was actually there! I glanced nervously up at the open doorway, to make sure no one was coming. None of the guys had stirred all night. Not one of them had used the bathroom.

We were so exposed! Screwing right there on the floor, in the middle of the living room. It scared me at first, that Rogan and Mason's doors were both open. They could walk out at any moment. They'd see us.

But that's also one of the things that excited me most. It made me hot to think one of them might be watching. That they might hear the sound of our bodies, our grunts and groans. The whimpers and moans I just couldn't control, as I squeezed down and came hard all over Desmond's magnificent dick…

I shifted beneath the covers, my legs falling slightly apart. Holy shit I was *wet*. Actually wet from reading this. And not just reading it, but thinking about Desmond. Imagining how big and 'magnificent' he might be, and what he might feel like inside *me*, rather than Emma.

A hand drifted down, and suddenly I was touching myself. Rubbing hard against the thin lace fabric of my panties, which were already soaking wet.

I read the rest of the entry with two fingers dipping in and out my own flower, imagining it was Desmond between my legs. He'd screwed Emma through two hard orgasms. Then he'd flipped her over, and dogged her hard from behind...

It was incredibly graphic. Like a sex-journal, written by someone who knew exactly what they were doing. I was torn between feeling admiration for this girl, who so eloquently put her experiences down on paper, and jealousy that *she* got to have Desmond... and not me.

That's crazy, Alyssa.

It was and it wasn't. I mean, I knew where I stood with Desmond. But at the same time, Emma was gone. And he was lonely. And so was I.

He came so hard, so fully inside me! It ran down my legs when he was finished, and my legs were trembling. Together we'd soaked the couch blanket beneath us. I had to throw it straight into the laundry room, or the others would know what we'd been doing on it.

My eyes closed. My fingers plunged.

Oh God...

My free hand slid down the flat of my belly, to flutter rapidly over my swollen button...

Fuuuuuckkkkkk!

I came hard, just like Emma had in her journal. Whimpering. Thrashing. Plunging three fingers in and out of myself while rubbing my clit, until I was gushing violently beneath the suddenly sweltering heat of the down comforter.

I lay there breathless for several moments, staring up at the ceiling. The same ceiling Emma stared at. The same bed Emma had slept in with Desmond, and probably done so *many*, many other things.

Still basking in my euphoric haze, I reached out and slid the book back into the nightstand. I'd only made it a few pages into the journal, and already I couldn't wait to read more. There was so much left.

And I had no doubt the other entries would be just as amazing.

Nine

ALYSSA

"Holy fucking SHIT!"

Mason blurted the words while flipping back his goggles, which were three-quarters covered in ice and powder. We were at the base of the mountain, chests heaving. Our cheeks rosy and red from the exhilarating run, all the way down.

"You're surprised?" I teased.

"Yes!" he exclaimed. "I mean... no, totally. But wow, yes!" He looked back at the final stretch of the run. Neither Rogan nor Desmond were even visible yet.

"I told you I'd beat you."

"I know, but—"

"But you thought you'd win because you're a guy?"

The question gave him pause. Enough hesitation that he just ended up shrugging.

"It's not about being a guy or a girl," I smiled back at

him. "I grew up skiing. My parents took us all the time."

"Yeah, okay. But—"

"I lived less than a half hour from Great Gorge," I went on. "I spent my entire teens there with friends, night-skiing, and the conditions were nothing like this powder. We skied on hard-packed *ice.* You learned to really stick your turns or you skidded into a tree. That's how it was."

People jostled past us, in line for the lift. Mason was looking at me admiringly now. His thick dark hair was plastered adorably over his head, all wet from melting snow.

"Plus... I might've been on the ski team in high school," I admitted coyly.

He laughed, and his whole gorgeous face came alive. "Oh shit."

"Yeah," I winked. "Let's not tell the others that part, though."

We'd started at the peak, taking Upper Nosedive into Midway into the Lower Liftline. Trail-wise, it was probably the fastest way down. The others had jumped off on a trail called Bypass, another black diamond. Either it slowed them down or they'd gotten lost, because right now it was just Mason and I.

"Let me ask you something," I said, feeling suddenly bold.

"Shoot."

"After our little rendezvous at the summer picnic..." I paused, watching his reaction carefully. "How come we never —"

"Hooked up?"

"Yeah. That."

Mason's wind-blasted face might've gone a little bit redder. It was difficult to tell.

"Well, to be honest I wasn't sure how you felt."

I reached out and poked him with one of my ski poles. "Really? Seriously?"

He looked uncomfortable. "I— I guess I mean—"

"After how hard I kissed you?"

He'd cast his emerald eyes downward, in the direction of our ski boots. It made him look cute. Almost sheepish.

"I was afraid," he said at last.

"Of what?"

"That you didn't mean to do it," he said simply. "We'd had more than a few beers together. And when we got back to the office on Monday, you acted like nothing happened."

"*You* acted like nothing happened!" I countered. "You wouldn't even *look* my way!"

Mason pulled four fingers through his tangle of wet hair and finally made eye contact with me. With the sun shining down on his sun-kissed face, he looked like the most gorgeous man on the planet.

"I didn't want to be pushy," he said with a shrug. "I was kinda waiting on you. And as time went on, I just guessed you weren't interested."

"So it's a case of..."

"Missed signals?"

I laughed, and my laughter came out as white puffs of smoke. "Well fuck me," I declared.

Mason grinned along with me. "Fuck both of us, really."

The conversation faltered, as our words sunk in. We were thinking about what they meant. What they *could* mean.

"So what's stopping you now?"

Whoa, Alyssa!

I couldn't believe I'd said it! It went directly against my pre-trip decision to let one of *them* make the first move.

"Who said anything's stopping me?" Mason challenged.

I slid closer, spreading my knees in a snowplow stance. Letting *his* skis go between *my* legs.

"I've thought about those kisses for almost six months," Mason admitted. As our bodies drew together, his voice went low. "How hot it was, back in that clearing. The feel of your body, writhing against me..."

"The taste of salt and sweat on our lips?" I teased.

"Hey," he smiled. "It was summer."

He edged closer, his skis sliding even deeper between my legs. The analogy wasn't lost on me.

"A *hot* summer," I practically whispered. Our breath was mingling now. We were that close.

"A very hot summer," he acknowledged. "And a very —"

"YO!"

We turned just in time to take face fulls of power, as Rogan skidded to a halt right beside us. Mason almost fell down. With his skis wedged so deeply between mine, he could barely separate them in time to maintain his balance.

"Tell us your beat her!"

Desmond swung up beside his friend, a split-second later. Their rosy cheeks and wet faces were looking expectantly at us.

"Wish I could," Mason smiled, shamefacedly. "She edged me out at the end, though."

I cleared my throat dramatically. "If by 'edged you out' you mean I was in the lift line for a half minute before you got here, then yes," I giggled, "you edged me out."

"Ski team," Mason said, jerking a thumb my way.

"Hey!"

"Sorry," he laughed.

I bumped him playfully with my hip. "I thought that was between you and me!"

"Some things yes," he winked. "That? No way."

"You know what this means, don't you?" said Desmond, shaking out his hat.

"I won the bet?"

"Yup."

"And what did I win again?"

"You get to pick what we're doing tonight," he said.

"Where we're going. Where we're eating, etc..."

"I thought we still had to shop?"

"We do," Rogan chimed in. "Big time."

"Then I vote we eat in," I said definitively. "We pick up some stuff for the house, and maybe I'll make dinner for you."

"Or maybe *we* make dinner for *you*," Rogan jumped in. "After all, you won the bet."

I pretended to consider it for a moment, knowing full well it was exactly what I wanted. Three hot guys, in the kitchen together. Cooking dinner for me, all at once.

"I could live with that."

"It's settled then," said Desmond, pulling his hat back on.

Mason and I shared a parting, secret look. One that spoke the promise that our conversation would be continued at a later date.

"Let's take the gondola to the other peak," he said, pointing over my shoulder. He elbowed Desmond and Rogan at the same time. "There might be some blue diamond trails there, so you guys can keep up with us."

Ten

ALYSSA

I thought watching the guys cook for me would be fun and relaxing. A great way to unwind after a long day on the slopes.

But I was only partially right.

It was fun for sure, but it was anything but relaxing. And that's because the three guys milling around our cabin's little kitchen were all sexy as hell.

You had Mason, stirring the sauce in a tight white T-shirt that showed off his bulging arms. Tasting it by swiping a finger across the wooden spoon, and then putting that finger in his mouth. I stood there, wine glass in hand. Wishing I could *be* that finger. Wanting to be the one he was tasting, as he winked back at me and added more salt.

Rogan was tending to a loaf of warm Italian bread, laying strips of roasted pepper and shredded bits from a ball of mozzarella cheese. He tore off a chunk and held it out to me, and as I leaned forward so he could feed me, the tip of his finger touched my outstretched tongue...

Damn.

And then there was Desmond, boiling the pasta. The broad-shouldered god I couldn't keep my eyes off of, no matter what I did. Since last night Desmond had gone up a few notches on my mental list, and he was already quite high. I kept picturing him naked, on the couch. Or on the floor in front of the fireplace, his broad, muscular back flexing and churning as he pumped his girlfriend full of his warm, wonderful seed.

The thoughts had me three times as flush as normal, and the guys had already noticed. I kept blaming it on the wine. Blaming it on a day of skiing against the cold winter wind, when in reality all I could think about was one thing:

Emma's journal.

Throughout our day together — as well as throughout our little shopping trip — my mind had wandered back to the little marbled book in my nightstand. I couldn't wait to get back to it. Couldn't wait to see what other events had happened here in the cabin, or even better, in my own bed.

We ate together, and dinner was delicious. The guys had outdone themselves in the kitchen, and in taking care of me too. The fire was roaring, the cabin warm. We were lounging around in the equivalent of our PJ's, and unless you went near the windows there still wasn't a hint of the cold, bitter weather that lurked just outside.

"So you have Christmas in this cabin every year," I noted, as we pushed our plates away.

"Pretty much," said Desmond. "One year we took two

weeks in Europe, and saw tons of stuff. And once we did Christmas on the beach," he smiled.

"Bermuda, I heard."

"Yup."

"Must've been a little too much like Florida," I said.

"Oh it was *way* better than Florida," said Mason. He leaned back in his chair and waved his arm around. "Still... not nearly as good as this."

As a Jersey girl, I had to agree. Christmas wasn't Christmas without a change of season. You needed the cold. And even better, the snow.

"In Australia right now it's the middle of summer," noted Rogan. "We should do that one year. Go down under."

Mason raised the bottle he was drinking. "Here's to *that.*"

I looked around, from wall to wall, rafter to rafter. Desmond was looking at me, so I looked back.

"So where are your decorations?"

He kept my gaze, while scratching at his sexy blond goatee. Between his stark blue eyes and his gorgeous smile, it made me want to eat him up.

"Don't you usually put stuff up?" I asked. "I mean, we're spending Christmas here, after all. Right?"

For a second or two he looked uncomfortable, and I wondered what was wrong. The guys exchanged awkward looks, and then Mason jumped in.

"Emma usually handled all that," he said flatly. "Not

to sound sexist or anything, but it was kind of her thing."

"Cool," I said, brushing it off. "Where's it all at?"

"Right there," said Desmond, jerking his chin skyward. "There's a whole bunch of stuff, up in the loft."

Eleven

ROGAN

It was fun, watching her work. Seeing her bounce happily around the cabin with all the Christmas decorations, while we kicked back and relaxed with beer and pretzels.

And God, she was so damned *sexy*, too. Her full pouty lips. Her pretty, girl-next-door face. I loved the way she flipped her hair as she went about her tasks, hanging wreaths and stringing lights. Setting up all the old decorations from the childhood Christmases Desmond spent here, while filled with that special joy and enthusiasm that only showed up in people around the holidays.

Her body was magnificent, especially out of her snow clothes. And she wore nothing special, really. A T-shirt and sweatpants, cut into a very short pair of shorts that showed off her long, toned legs.

"Is this straight?"

Desmond took another pull from his bottle before answering.

"Lean out a little more," he told her playfully. "I can't tell yet."

Alyssa's mouth scrunched into a 'ha ha' frown, but she did what he asked. She was up in the loft, hanging onto the balcony with one arm. Trying to straighten out one of the decorations high over the cabin's doorway, while balancing on one slender, well-tanned leg.

"Now turn," said Mason.

"I can't turn it."

"Not the decoration," he laughed. "*You.* Turn in toward the wall a little, so you can reach better."

She stopped, leaving the decorating where it was to place a hand on her hip. "I'm starting to think this was straight all along," she said. "And you just want to see my ass."

"Maybe," Mason shrugged.

I laughed, and we all laughed together. We were doing a lot of that this trip, laughing together. Which reminded me...

... *of Emma.*

"Okay, it looks good enough," said Desmond.

"The wreath," Alyssa challenged. "Or my ass?"

"Both, really."

"Alright then," she giggled, climbing nimbly down the wooden ladder. "As long as we have that settled."

Damn she was beautiful. So curvy and feminine, with that cornsilk auburn hair spilling down the center of her back. I wondered absently if it would reach her ass. I wondered even more how my fists would feel wrapped up in it, my fingers sifting slowly through that shimmering, curly sea.

Last night I'd had to walk away from the conversation in her bedroom. Hell I'd just about spurned her, for Alyssa's would-be invitation to keep her warm.

And damn, it was one of the hardest things I'd ever done.

I was frustrated as hell at our 'deal'. Shit, I regretted ever making it in the first place. My own stupidity kept me up all night, tossing and turning. Kicking myself for not taking things a step or two further, while Mason snored blissfully from the other side of the bed.

You could just break it, you know...

It was damn tempting. Almost as tempting as she was. The guys would be pissed of course, but eventually they'd understand. Originally I figured it would be simple to keep things platonic, and then make my move once we got back home. But now...

Now I felt a sense of urgency. Not just in my need to be with her again, but in the fact that Mason would be spending the whole trip with a girl he'd already been to first base with. If there was still an attraction there, it could blossom during the trip. And there I'd be, hanging back like an idiot. Sitting on my hands, with both thumbs up my ass...

And of course there was Desmond, too. I could see the way he was looking at her. It was a look I'd seen all too many times before, on all of our trips. Only back then...

Back then, it was more than okay.

Yes. Yes it was.

And you know exactly why.

I finished my beer and got up to grab another. Alyssa bounced past me, all smiles. My nostrils picked up a gentle whiff of something flowery and sweet. Something that set the rest of my senses alive and tingling, like they'd been in her room last night.

Maybe I'd go to her later on. Wait for the others to fall asleep, and creep down to her bedroom to see if she were still up.

I might be risking the wrath of the others, but they'd only be mad because they hadn't moved first. And of course, another possibility also existed:

The three of us could form a midnight traffic jam in the hallway.

Twelve

ALYSSA

After eight hours on the mountain — followed by all the running around — the four of us were physically exhausted. Desmond was falling asleep on the couch. Mason, staring numbly into the fire. Rogan and I had played two games of checkers, courtesy of some timeworn box I'd found up in the loft. So far we were one and one. Even Steven.

Tomorrow promised to be a big day. We were going to explore Stowe together. Take in the quaint little sleepy town, and then hit the nightlife later on, closer to the base of the mountain.

It was the perfect excuse to retire for the night.

An hour later the cabin was dark and silent, except for the warm, flickering fire. I was tucked away beneath the blankets, Emma's journal already in hand. I opened it to the next entry, and started to read.

I couldn't wait for tonight. For what was about

to happen.

Apparently it skipped right past the day's events, and launched straight into the good stuff. Which was okay by me.

We'd talked about it. We'd fantasized about it for weeks. And now all of sudden, tonight… it was finally about to happen. The butterflies pounded against the insides of my stomach. Almost enough to make me nauseous.

Intrigued, I read through the initial details of their encounter. It was all taking place here in this room, in this very bed. Emma was going down on Desmond. Bringing him hard in her mouth, and then climbing on and impaling herself on him.

He felt bigger than ever inside of me Hard as steel, and so achingly thick. I spread my hands over his chest and lowered myself all the way down, taking him to the root. Not stopping until he was buried all the way, and then pausing to savor the feeling of wholeness that came with being packed so wonderfully full.

A familiar heat rose up inside me, starting at my very core. I was feeling the butterflies myself. But I couldn't keep my eyes away. Couldn't keep them from crawling the journal, uninterrupted, in the cold, filtered moonlight:

I rode him for five minutes, maybe ten. It seemed like forever, though. The anticipation of what was about to happen had me wetter than I'd been in my life. I knew what we'd do... I just didn't know when, or how, or under what circumstances. I only knew that I wanted *it. Wanted it more than I'd wanted anything in my whole life.*

And I could see, looking down into his eyes... that he wanted it as well.

Desmond's hands stayed on my hips, pushing and pulling me up and down on his manhood. Working me into such a frenzy, I could hear my own wetness. He leaned forward, mashing his face against my breasts. Sucking one and then the other; teasing them between his lips, tracing them with his tongue as I continued riding him closer and closer to the inevitable edge...

And just when I was about to explode? He pushed me downward. I cried out as he shoved me away from his beautiful cock, his hands guiding my shoulders until I was kneeling between his legs again. And then I was blowing him, all the way down. Tasting my wetness up and down his entire length, as his fingers sifted through my hair and his hands rolled themselves into two tight fists...

I was face down. Ass up. Sucking my boyfriend

hard and fast, as he guided my head with both hands. And then I heard it; the door, creaking open behind me. At least, it could've been the door. It could've also been my imagination.

Only it wasn't.

I managed to glance up, straight into his eyes. I needed the affirmation, but Desmond was already looking over my shoulder. My heart was pounding now! My stomach was tied up in knots. Somehow I kept my cool, kept working at the task at hand...

And that's when I felt two strange hands settle over my hips.

I think I sighed, or moaned out loud. I don't even remember. All I recall was stopping to glance back, to see which of them it actually was. I remember looking into Rogan's eyes, as he settled in behind me. Noting the smooth nakedness of his beautifully-muscled body, and then swinging my attention back to my boyfriend's own lust-filled gaze.

Desmond rolled his fists, guiding my mouth back over the head of his thickness. I was too far gone to do anything but obey. I took him deep, my whole body shaking with arousal...

... and that's when his friend slowly pushed his cock into my pussy...

Thirteen

ALYSSA

Holy shit! I couldn't believe it!

I read it again, and again after that. Each time, my mouth dropped open even wider. Each reading made me *that* much more wet.

They were sharing her.

The revelation was astonishing, but also unspeakably hot. I held the journal now in two trembling hands. I felt a rush of adrenaline. The same knots of excitement Emma must have felt, in the pit of my stomach.

No wonder why she always went on the trip with them!

A log cracked loudly, back in the fire. I glanced fearfully through the open door, into the hallway. But no one was there.

I thought back to everything I knew of Emma, back when she was still with the company. She was a cute little brunette. Kinda quiet, a little shy. She was already dating Desmond by the time I'd been hired. He'd only recently been promoted from working the construction sites to overlooking jobs in the office.

Emma? I thought to myself, suddenly wide awake. She didn't seem the type.

Emma... screwing Desmond and *Rogan.*

I opened the book back to where my thumb had saved the page. The entry wasn't done. Not even close.

It was a little crazy, how easily it had all happened. How quickly we'd gone from bedroom fantasy to stark reality. But that was it — it was happening. Rogan was actually fucking me. Taking me deep and slow from behind, while I sucked on my boyfriend and rocked back and forth between them.

And it felt absolutely incredible.

It took a few minutes to let go, and to really enjoy it. I didn't even realize I'd been tensing up. Then Desmond began massaging my shoulders, my body relaxed. He sat up and took my face in his two big, gentle hands. And then suddenly he was kissing me. Kissing and tonguing me hotly, while his friend dug his hands into my hips and screwed me from behind.

That was my favorite part — the way he held me as his own. He took one of my hands and interlaced our fingers, while whispering in my ear that it was okay. I started screwing back. Giving myself permission as the last of the guilt fled my mind. And then the whispers began getting nastier. Dirtier. And I started growing even wetter just thinking about the things Desmond was saying to me; the things they'd do to me. The positions he wanted to try. All the perverted acts that were now opened up to us, that he needed me to perform.

And I knew right then I wanted it all.

I had to stop for a moment. My pulse was screaming, my mouth was bone dry. My hand — having a mind of its own — wanted to wander again. To travel south, to the place that might bring me even a fraction of the same pleasure Emma was experiencing here in her journal.

I read on while she detailed her thoughts, her feelings. The gut-churning conflict going on in her mind, being held and kissed by her boyfriend... as one of his best friends had his way with her.

And apparently, *loving* it.

Rogan was going harder now, faster and deeper. Screwing himself against my ass in tight, sexy circles. And then all at once he stopped and stiffened, and I knew what was about to happen. I looked up into Desmond's eyes, and he told me:

"Let him come in you."

I'm squirming now, even as I write this. Because

let me tell you there's nothing — and I mean absolutely nothing — on the whole planet that can prepare you for how hot it is to have your loving boyfriend tell *you to take another man's come inside you...*

Rogan exploded a moment later, and I came right with him. Squeezing him as I felt him contract. Screwing my eyes shut, as he pumped me full of his warm, sticky seed. Desmond kissed my face, over and over again. My cheeks. My chin. My forehead.

It was sweet and *sexy. And right then, it was the greatest thing in the entire world.*

I was rubbing hard now, three fingers deep in my own throbbing entrance. Imagining my womb was Emma's, overflowing with Rogan's come. That her pleasure was my pleasure, too. I was slipping downward, beneath the sheets and comforter.

And then the next paragraph knocked me clear back into the headboard again.

They turned me over together, sliding me onto my back. Placing their hands on the insides of my thighs, and spreading my legs wide. That's when I looked up and saw Mason, standing there in the doorway... and my heart skipped its next series of beats.

His shirt was already off. I'd seen that before of course, but now he was untying the string on his sweatpants, while staring directly into my eyes. I felt naked and exposed before him, but only for a moment. Then I remembered our deal — that it was going to be all or nothing — and I crooked a finger his way, beckoning him over as Desmond still held me in his warm, naked lap.

Those sweatpants dropped, revealing only more nakedness beneath. Nothing but the thick, heavy-looking manhood that dangled between his legs.

And then he was on the bed. Crawling between my thighs and stroking himself with one big, gorgeous arm. I lost sight of him as Desmond bent down, and then suddenly I was being kissed again. Kissed by my boyfriend and *Rogan, together, as one.*

They took turns making out with me, while running their hands all over my body. They were cupping my breasts. Rolling my areolae between their thumbs, as I grabbed their heads and pulled them so hard against my lips that every breath I took belonged to them as well.

They kissed me over and over again until I finally felt it: the head of Mason's manhood, being dragged up and down through the shallows of my sex. It felt bigger than the others. And so wonderfully, impossibly thick as it pushed its way in…

I dropped the journal, shoving my fingers home one

last time as my whole body began to convulse. The ensuing climax was mind-erasing. I literally forgot *everything* else, as my brain flooded with an ocean of sweet endorphins that swept all but the pure distilled pleasure of my rushing orgasm from my lust-fueled brain.

Fuuuuuuuck!

I came two times in rapid succession — something that had only happened once or twice in my life. I found myself clawing the sheets with my free hand. Thrashing desperately beneath the comforter, as I wound slowly down from the fluffy white heaven of cloud nine.

It was crazy. No, it was ludicrous!

But it had actually *happened*, all of it. And it happened here. In this very cabin, with these very men. The same three men who'd invited me along on their trip, and who'd been flirting with me the whole time.

And with whom I'd been flirting shamelessly back.

Fourteen

ALYSSA

"Ah, *there* she is!"

I stumbled into the kitchen to the smell of sizzling bacon, my robe clenched tightly around my body. Someone handed me a cup of coffee. Someone else, a spatula.

"Can you finish off the pancakes?" asked Desmond with a smile.

I took a long pull of coffee before answering. Heavy milk, a little sugar. They'd gotten it right.

"I think so."

"Good," he said, pointing to the pan. "Now get to work."

Mason was scrambling a batch of eggs, adding milk for fluffiness instead of a splash of water. I'd have to teach him, but not now. Rogan was laying strips of bacon on a plate covered in paper towels. All three guys were moving with purpose — probably because the coffee pot was already empty.

They also seemed to be in a really great mood.

"You should've woke me," I mumbled. "I feel bad."

"We figured we'd let you sleep in," said Rogan. "Beauty sleep, and all that."

"Yeah, but—"

"But nothing," said Desmond. "You were probably exhausted from out-skiing us all day yesterday." He nodded toward the pan. "Better flip those."

I yawned and flipped the pancakes, noticing I was already thirty seconds too late. Oh well. There was still more batter.

It wasn't the pancakes I was focusing on, though.

No, all I could think about was last night. Emma's journal. What was in it...

Unbelievable.

My gaze flitted from Desmond to Rogan, and to Mason, too. I was looking at them with all new eyes, now. It was like seeing three different people — men I'd never even met before. And yet they were the same three beautiful co-workers who I'd been friends with, flirted with, even made out with, over the past couple of years.

Only now...

Now I kept envisioning them doing the things in that journal. I pictured Desmond, holding Emma's face in his two big hands. Kissing her like a lover, while Rogan drilled his girlfriend from behind. I kept picturing Mason, standing in the doorway. Stroking his himself up and down as he climbed onto the bed...

"Trash those," Desmond laughed at my pancakes. "Here. Let me wash the pan out."

I handed it over numbly, studying his face. Imagining the look in his eyes as he watched his girlfriend do all those crazy things.

They shared her. All three of them.

I still couldn't believe it. Only also, I could.

They took turns on her. Passed her body back and forth, between them.

I'd read on a little more, after my orgasm. Enough at least, to see how the rest of the night had played out. Desmond had watched as Mason spread Emma wide, plowing her until she was almost begging for mercy. Screwing her until he couldn't hold back, and then emptied himself inside her just as Rogan had done.

And then afterward, Desmond had pinned her down by the wrists. Pushed himself back inside, and taken his own turn. The others had stayed and watched, resting along either side of her. Leisurely, they'd played with her body. Kissed her softly, endlessly, while her boyfriend screwed her slow and deep.

The night ended with a third load deep in Emma's belly, and then the two of them cuddling under the sheets. With the others retired back to their rooms, she'd told him how much she'd enjoyed the whole thing. Thanked him for fulfilling her fantasy, which he pointed out had been *their* fantasy, together.

And then said something else that made my stomach flutter, right before the entry ended.

Emma said she couldn't wait to do it *again.*

"Here," said Desmond, handing me back a clean, shiny pan. "Butter that thing up and let's go. Eggs are almost done."

I swallowed hard. For some reason there was a lump in my throat.

You know the reason.

Mechanically I went through the motions of preparing the next batch of pancakes. But I couldn't help myself. I was stealing sideways glances at the others. Imagining them all screwing Desmond's girlfriend together, writhing hotly between her legs.

Three years.

I remembered the date of the journal's entry. That alone was astounding.

They've been sharing her for three years!

Two and a half at least, I thought to myself. Desmond and Emma had broken up before the summer even started. Then again, I hadn't read any more, so I didn't know for sure if they even did it again. It's possible it was a one-shot deal. The fulfillment of a long-time fantasy. But the way Emma talked about it...

Well, I sure didn't think so.

"Those look good," said Desmond, nodding toward the three perfect pancakes I'd recently flipped. "Plate em' up, already. Let's eat."

A minute later I was taking my spot at the little round table, studying the guys over the rim of my coffee mug. They were laughing and carrying on. Needling each other, and elbowing me for a reaction. The same kind of things they'd always done, and I'd always laughed along with them.

Only now there were a whole flock of butterflies bouncing around in my stomach.

Fifteen

ALYSSA

Stowe was every bit as beautiful as in all the photos I'd seen, and I'd seen quite a few. But right now, around the holidays...

Well, things were on a whole different level.

The small, sleepy town centered around the convergence of three main roads. The houses were mostly old colonials. Each one decorated warmly from within, and brilliantly on the outside with Christmas lights of every conceivable size and color.

During the day the place was breathtakingly beautiful. Every little home and shop was decorated to the nines. A pine tree on almost every front lawn was strung with twinkling lights, all the way down to the looming presence of the huge ski resort, high up on the mountain.

At night everything glowed, reflected by the layers of ice and bright white snow. We drove around for quite a while, enjoying each other's company while we took in the sights.

Sipping hot chocolate in the spacious old truck, while keeping warm beneath our thick winter coats.

"I'm starving," Rogan finally stated.

Mason raised his arm. "I second that notion."

Desmond laughed from behind the wheel. "All in favor of Harrison's?"

The four of us chimed in at once, and the truck swung around. We'd passed the cool-looking bar and restaurant ten minutes back. Since then we'd been ogling photos and reviews online — the place seemed warm and inviting, and had fantastic-looking burgers.

We sat at the bar for almost an hour while waiting for a table, but I didn't mind one bit. The place was gorgeous. Its stained wood-timber construction stretched in every direction, while we split a pitcher of beer and awaited our booth.

"The cabin looks beautiful by the way," Desmond said to me. "You did a bang-up job."

"I try," I smiled. "It's still missing one thing though."

"And what's that?"

I shook my head as I licked the foam from my upper lip. "Isn't it obvious? A Christmas tree!"

Mason leaned against the bar, staring my way. He'd been giving me once-overs and half-smiles all night. Nothing bad, but it felt almost like he *knew* something. Something I didn't.

"There's a pre-lit Christmas tree up in the loft," said Rogan. "Didn't you see it?"

"I did."

He raised an eyebrow. "And?"

"And it looked like the first plastic tree ever made," I chuckled. "Shot out of a cannon."

Mason laughed, even as Desmond's face went a little wounded.

"What do you mean?" asked Desmond. "We used that tree all through my childhood!"

"She's right though," said Mason. "That thing is... well..."

"Ratty?" Rogan inquired casually.

"Yeah. And that's being nice about it."

Desmond frowned, but I squeezed his arm comfortingly. "It's no big deal," I said. "We can use that one if you really want to. Or..."

I let the words trail off, as something else came to mind.

"Or what?"

"Never mind," I said. "You let me take care of all that. The tree's on me."

"On you?" asked Mason.

"Yeah, I've got something of a plan," I admitted. "I might need the truck though," I said, turning to Desmond.

He looked at me skeptically. "Can you *drive* the truck?"

I laughed merrily. "In Jersey, half of us are born on the Parkway. The other half come out with two hands on the steering wheel."

"Yikes," said Mason, envisioning my boast.

"Just wait till' tomorrow," I said. "You'll see. Leave the tree to me."

We toasted tomorrow, and drained our glasses just in time to be shown to our booth. Dinner was excellent. The company, even more. With each passing hour things felt even more casual, more relaxed. The alcohol didn't hurt of course, but the guys themselves were just fun to hang out with.

In time, I even forgot about last night.

We started up about work first, and that led to a dozen hilarious stories, each one funnier than the last. Mason had some *interesting* business trips with some very strange people. Desmond told tales of being on site, and some of the wonderfully stupid things clients did. Rogan's stores all took place within the office, featuring people we knew. I got dirt on a lot of people. And as the drinks flowed, I even gave dirt too.

The thing that struck me though, was how fluid everything was between them. These men had been friends for a long time, long before I'd left Jersey and made my way down to Florida. They jumped in on each other's stories. Finished each other's sentences. And they got along like brothers, even when it seemed they were mercilessly poking fun at each other.

It was obvious they'd be sharing each other's lives for a long time. Which, in the back of my mind, seemed to justify — at least a little bit, anyway — how they could be sharing something as taboo as a woman, too.

Eventually we all stumbled out into the snow, which by now was coming down hard. Desmond had quit drinking hours ago, after only a couple of beers. He started up the big truck as we all climbed in, and pointed us in the direction of

Stowe mountain.

"Still want to hit the lodge tonight?"

It had been our original plan: to finish out the day by checking out the nightlife at the base of the mountain. Only now...

"Maybe tomorrow?" Mason offered.

He was sitting in the back seat with me, our bodies leaning heavily into each other. For warmth maybe, sure. But also just for the comfort of being close.

"I'm with you," said Rogan. "We've been running around town all day. Let's save the lodge for another night."

In the darkness of the backseat, Mason's hand found mine. "Besides," he said, "the *real* party's always been in our cabin anyway."

I relaxed my hand, letting his fingers interlace with mine. Mason shot me that sideways glance again. His eyes flashed dangerously in the dim light, as he gave me a gentle squeeze.

"Home it is, then," said Desmond, swinging the truck around.

Sixteen

MASON

I loved everything about her. Her heart. Her wit. The way she was always flipping her hair back, right before she laughed. All of it — she was the whole package.

And then of course there was last night...

"I say it's Colonel Mustard, in the study, with the revolver."

She looked from one of us to the other, her eyes alight with growing excitement. Batting those ridiculously long eyelashes, while no one said a thing.

"Nothing to say now, eh?" Alyssa laughed. "No more tough talk. No more big flowery speeches about being the best?"

Desmond dropped his cards. So did I. Alyssa reached gleefully into the center of the board, and pulled the cards out of the secret envelope. One by one she turned them over.

Colonel Mustard. The study...

The *rope.*

"Damn," she swore, her face going crestfallen. "What the—"

Rogan smiled devilishly and held up the revolver card. Alyssa growled.

"I *asked* you for the revolver three turns ago!"

"No you didn't."

"Yes I did!"

Rogan laughed. "Oh yeah? Prove it."

Alyssa jumped abruptly over the board and tackled him, nearly spilling her wine. Desmond reached out at the last second and caught it, just as they rolled playfully across the floor.

Things had definitely progressed to a more intimate setting, since our night began. We'd played a beat-up game of Pictionary, but it hadn't been fair. With Alyssa and I on 'Team Architect', we'd destroyed the others. Plus, as it turned out, she could *really* draw.

We'd tried Chinese Checkers, but no one could remember the rules, and half the marbles were missing. Rogan had suggested we play 'strip Yahtzee', until Desmond shot him a dirty look.

"We are *not* stripping to Yahtzee," our host had declared.

I'd laughed and pointed out I didn't even know it was *possible* to strip to Yahtzee. But Alyssa had smiled mischievously and said it was too bad. She claimed she would've seriously considered it, because the 'odds were in her favor'.

Right now Rogan was on top of her, pinning her down. They were nose to nose, face to face. I had to admit, I was getting a little jealous.

"I can't find her tickle spot," Rogan grunted.

"Maybe you're not looking in the right places?" teased Alyssa.

He let go of her wrists, sliding his hands under her armpits. She went instantly wild, laughing and flailing, her hair thrashing wildly over her giggling face.

My thoughts wandered back to last night. To our *almost* rendezvous, that had ended abruptly with me standing in the hallway...

Holy shit.

I'd spent almost an hour in bed, staring up at the ceiling. Debating whether or not I should go see her. It meant betraying the guys of course, but ultimately I felt like I should get first shot. After all, I was the one who'd kissed her. I was the one she admitted having an attraction to, during our conversation at the base of the mountain.

It was nothing to creep out into the hallway once Rogan fell asleep. But right at the doorway to her room...

Well, that's when I'd seen something that blew me completely away.

"Alright alright," she shouted. "I give up!"

They untangled, slowly, and the two of them sat up. Rogan reached for his beer. Alyssa pinned her hair back behind both ears, while Desmond handed back her wine.

"You're kinda fun," smiled Rogan. "You know that?"

Alyssa took a long pull from her glass. Pleasantly tipsy, and with her hair all fluffed out, she looked sexy as hell.

"As fun as *Emma?*" she dared ask.

The room went abruptly silent. While the fire crackled away, Rogan and I exchanged worried looks.

"Sorry..." Alyssa said immediately. She turned to Desmond. "I— I didn't mean to—"

"Even more fun," Desmond said at last. He forced a broad smile. "Seriously."

Rogan's shoulders relaxed. I heaved an inner sigh of relief.

"No, you're just being nice," Alyssa corrected herself. "I really shouldn't have said that."

"Why?" I asked. "Aren't *you* having fun?"

"Me? I'm having the time of my life," she answered eagerly. "You guys have been nothing but amazing to me. I— I guess I'm just a little insecure," she explained. "I know you did this trip with Emma a bunch of times, and I wanted to make sure I was... well... fitting in."

"You're fitting in," said Rogan. He clinked his bottle against her glass. "Trust us."

"You're the better game player for sure," I said with a smile.

"And the best wrestler," Rogan added.

"And the best decorator," said Desmond, waving an arm around. The twinkling Christmas lights strung all around the room added a holiday feel to everything we were doing. "Much better than Emma ever was."

I saw her go red with all the attention, but it was a good look. An honest look.

"Aww, that's all very nice," she smiled. "But what about you guys?"

We looked back at her together, not understanding.

"Who's the best at what?"

Rogan chimed in right away. He pounded his chest with one fist. "Well I'm *clearly* the best cook."

Desmond and I shot him a look that said his claim might be debatable. But we let him have it anyway.

"I'm the best-looking," Desmond grinned. He struck a pose, stroking his goatee for effect. Alyssa laughed.

"And of course I'm the best kisser," I said proudly. I looked straight at her and winked, in full view of the other guys.

"Bullshit," Desmond and Rogan said at the same time.

We all chuckled a little, as the cabin fell silent again. Alyssa was staring back at us strangely, almost impishly. But in a good way

"Well, I could tell you that right now."

All three of us were frozen where we sat. You could hear a pin drop.

"Tell us what?"

"Who's the best kisser, silly," Alyssa giggled. "I'm willing to settle that for you, give my honest opinion. For science, of course," she added hastily.

The silence stretched out for what seemed like a long time. Alyssa stared back at us over her wine glass, all long hair and sexy green eyes.

"It would have to be an *objective* opinion," said Desmond abruptly.

"Of course."

"No favoritism," said Rogan. "Plus... well, we all know you already kissed Mason."

My heart was pounding faster as her eyes flitted to me. "That was six months ago," Alyssa said. "Are you really afraid I'll remember his lips?"

"Wait," I jumped in. "Are you saying my kisses are forgettable?"

"Oh, no," she giggled with mock innocence. "I would *never* say that!"

"A blindfold then."

Desmond's suggestion stopped us all in our tracks. I could barely believe he was doing this. He'd been the one to suggest our little pact.

"Are you willing to do that?" Rogan asked.

Alyssa shrugged. "Sure. I guess so. What kind of kiss are we talking about?"

"Lips only," said Desmond. "No other touching."

"That's not what I meant," Alyssa replied. "I mean... a one-shot kiss? Or a *kiss* kiss?"

"You mean a makeout kiss," I said. "Lips, tongue,

everything."

She took another sip of wine and nodded slowly. "It's the only way to really judge, don't you think?"

God, she was so hot right now! All flush and warm and full-lipped. Staring back at us demurely, from her corner of the couch.

"A time-limit then," said Desmond, "rather than a kiss limit. Let's say, thirty seconds."

She placed a slender finger against her face and tilted her head, pretending to think.

"A minute would be nicer."

The way she was negotiating only turned me on even more. I could see it was the same for Desmond. Rogan too.

"Alright," said Desmond. "One minute."

Alyssa's pretty mouth spread into a sly smile. Rising from the couch, she set her wine glass down on the coffee table and pushed it away.

"Go get the blindfold then," she said demurely.

Seventeen

ALYSSA

The kiss was slow, sensual. Deep and beautiful. A pair of firm, masculine lips rotating softly against mine, as my whole body melted into a boiling puddle of heat and sex.

Oh. My. God.

I was ten seconds in. Or thirty. Or maybe an hour. I couldn't even tell! There was only the sensation of being held, without being touched. Of being possessed, without any other connection but our two hungry mouths—

Beep-beep-beep! Beep-beep-beep!

The alarm on the phone went off, signaling it was over. One hot minute. Sixty scorching seconds of a full-blown makeout session, cut short by the 'rules' of our little kissing game.

DAMN!

The lips reluctantly broke from mine — maybe even pulled away, as one of the others broke us up. I couldn't tell which it was, and that's because I was blindfolded. In total darkness.

I swallowed, trying to compose myself. Wondering when the next contestant would step forward, ready to upstage his previous competitor. My lips were ready. My body was willing...

And that's when a hand slid behind me, cupping my ass.

Ohhhh...

My body stiffened.

Ohhhh wow.

Even as it wanted to go totally, blissfully limp.

What the—

I heard a slap — the sound of skin against skin. The hand on my ass squeezed involuntarily for one glorious second, and then it was quickly slapped away from my body by someone else.

No touching, remember? It's against the rules.

A mouth closed over mine. The kiss was more insistent than the last, but no less passionate. A tongue pushed past my lips and slid past my teeth, seeking my own tongue, like some lost but well-loved playmate.

Our noses brushed, as we turned into each other. I felt the soft tickle of a goatee...

Desmond! I thought to myself. *Or maybe Rogan...*

The anonymous lips churned hard against mine, our mouths becoming one in the quest for mutual pleasure.

Kissing blindfolded was like nothing I'd ever experienced before. There was something about denying one sense that seemed to heighten the others. Make everything *that* much more intense, especially since my hands were proverbially tied as well.

I could feel myself getting insanely turned on. The raw, visceral emotions of lust and need and desire — fueled by the buzz I already had going — were all magnified by the blindfold. Not to mention the idea that I really didn't know which one of the guys was on the giving end of this much pleasure. Only that I'd get all three of them, each in turn.

Just like Emma...

The thought was a stab of arousal, deep in my belly. Emma had done this. I was following in her footsteps. Even if they were just baby steps, it was still—

Beep-beep-beep! Beep-beep-beep!

The tongue in my mouth swirled hard, one last time. Drawing me in. Literally stealing my breath away in one last kiss, delivered with the urgency of two lovers about to part at an airport, or a train station.

Our lips disengaged, and suddenly there was a presence before me. I could smell cologne. Or maybe aftershave. The sweet, delicious musk of a man, only which man I still didn't know.

And then a pair of hands went to my face, pulling me in. Kissing me while caressing my cheeks, the fingertips soft and slow and wonderful.

"Ahem!"

Off to the side, one of the guys loudly cleared their

throat. The hands on my face disappeared, even as I went to hold them in mine.

Crap.

The no-touching rule was regrettable. I should've negotiated better. Then again, could I really complain? At the moment I was doing just fine. Making out with the softest, most wonderful pair of lips, while a strong, confident tongue slid sensually against mine.

My body was on fire. Every inch of my skin was goosebumps. And down between my legs...

The way my thighs rubbed together, I could tell I was already *sopping* wet.

Emma did this.

That thought again. Pervasive. Gut-churning.

She did a lot more than this.

I was crossing a line. It was a line I'd invited myself to step over, sure, but it was a line nonetheless. And yet I found I didn't care. I hadn't been kissed like this in months, years — maybe even ever, in my entire life. I *needed* this. But even as I confronted the honesty of that realization, I knew something else too:

That I wanted a lot *more* than just kissing.

Beep-beep-beep! Beep-beep-beep!

My heart sank as I realized the fun was over. This time it was I who wouldn't pull back. It was I who stood on my toes, following that wonderful connection as the last of my coworkers pulled back from our little experiment.

Then the lips I'd been kissing leaned in quickly,

pushing themselves against my ear.

"I saw what you did last night..."

The words were barely audible, just above a whisper. But they were unmistakable. And they sent a shiver of panic — or was it actually excitement — bolting straight through me.

What I did...

I didn't even have time to gasp. Someone took me by both my shoulders. They spun me slowly around two, three, maybe four times. It was impossible to count. I was already dizzy from all the kissing.

... last night.

"Annnnd... there we go!"

One of the men removed the blindfold, and there I was. Standing between all three of them. I was the *bottle* in the middle of the sexiest game of spin the bottle that had ever been realized.

"So who was it?" Rogan asked with a flourish. "Number one? Number two?"

"Or number three?" Mason finished for him.

"W—Who was *what?*" I stammered. My legs were so wobbly I could barely stand. I reached out with one hand, feeling for the couch.

"The best kisser!" Desmond exclaimed. "The whole reason we just did that!"

Mason let out a low chuckle. "*One* of the reasons, anyway," he mumbled under his breath.

They were staring at me now, arms crossed. Hands on

their hips. I knew this was for some pretty big bragging rights. That I was about to make one of these guys *very* happy, and the other two extremely jealous.

"I... umm..."

Desmond arched an eyebrow. The others merely shifted.

"I probably need another round," I said quickly. "One minute is too fast to tell anything. Three minutes would be better. And maybe if I were on the couch, you know? Lying down, or—"

Beneath his sexy blond goatee, Desmond's smile was almost reluctant.

"Oh no," he said. "I think you've had enough kissing for one night."

My shoulders slumped. *Damn.*

"Maybe we could revisit this when you're... in better shape?" he suggested with a wink.

Behind him stood the others, all nodding their agreement. I felt woozy. Dreamy. Flush and warm.

"C'mon," Rogan said, taking me by the hand. He jerked his chin, and Mason took the other — more for stability than anything else. "Let's get you tucked in."

Suddenly the hallways seemed very long, my bed very far away. It also seemed like a good idea. I nodded.

"Tomorrow's another day."

Eighteen

ALYSSA

The truck bounced over the next rise, and me along with it. It was a lot of fun, driving such a big vehicle. It made me feel powerful, being that high off the road. Having the weight of so much steel beneath me.

I was bringing back breakfast — four egg sandwiches that looked pretty close to decent — but that wasn't all. I'd also fulfilled my promise. I'd woken earlier than all three of the others, which led me to believe they'd stayed up even after they put me to bed. They probably drank a couple more beers, enjoying their time together. Possibly even talking about what had happened...

Oh they definitely *talked about what happened.*

A wave of heat surged through me as I remembered last night. Getting close with them. Wrestling with Rogan on the carpeted floor. And then afterward...

Afterward I'd kissed them — all three men. Or rather they'd kissed *me*. The whole thing had been almost like a dream — slow and sensual. But they'd also kissed me long and hard, with every ounce of passion they could. Pulling out all the stops.

And they'd done it in front of each other.

That was the part of the memory that gave me residual goosebumps: that the three of them had done this before. They didn't know *I* knew it, and that only excited me even more. They'd done these same things with Emma, and in the same room to boot. Only they'd gone much, much further...

How far are you willing to go, Alyssa?

It was a fair question. Between how indescribably hot last night had been, and the incredible things found in Emma's journal, giving myself over to the guys was just about all I could think about. And yet, I wasn't anyone's girlfriend. I was merely a coworker they'd invited last minute. Each of them had their own professional relationship with me, but that's as far as it went. Until last night, anyway.

And what would they think of you afterward?

That was the problem, really. Falling into bed with them might be easy, especially knowing they'd done this before. I'd flipped through some more of the journal in my nightstand, and had read about all kinds of things they'd done with Emma over the many trips they had together.

It wasn't a one-shot deal. It wasn't a singular fantasy.

The three of them had been screwing the shit out of this lucky bitch every Christmas for the last three years.

But with me, how would it go? Kissing was one thing, but if I slept with them.. would they still respect me the way they did now?

We'd return to work for the new year, and there would be all these sideways glances. People in the office, cracking jokes about how one of the most single girls took a secluded vacation with three of the hottest, most eligible office bachelors. Even if they didn't *know* what was up... they'd know what was up.

My heart beat faster just thinking about it. Me... and *three guys.* Three incredibly hot, charming, beautiful men, who'd already been showering me with positive attention. Three guys who would suddenly be showering me with something *else.*

Holy shit.

They were gentlemen, that much I knew. I was pretty sure they could keep their mouths shut. But *we'd* know. The four of us. And not having the advantage of being someone's girlfriend, I'm not sure I'd command the same level of automatic respect that Emma had.

Still, I wanted them. Oh, *God* how I wanted them. But I also didn't want to lose the fun office rapport we currently had.

You want to eat your cake and have it too.

Yeah. I guess I did.

I rolled on, thinking about the guys. Trying to figure out who'd kissed me first and who'd cupped my ass. Which of the three of them had whispered in my ear that they'd actually *seen* what I'd done the night before. That alone should've alarmed me, but strangely enough, it only served to turn me on.

The butterflies were back in stomach again. I wanted

Desmond to crush me beneath his perfect chest. For Rogan to sweep me into his rock-hard arms, and hold me steady while Mason prepared to enter me with the swollen head of his apparently thick—

Could you really do it?

The thought jumped into my head, just as the snow-covered driveway leapt in front of me. I almost missed the turn! I jerked the wheel just in time to bounce onto the winding stretch of snow-covered pavement that led up to the cabin itself.

It was picture perfect. Something out of an oil painting really, complete with icicles and frosted windows and a little curl of smoke wafting up from the brick chimney.

The front door opened at the sound of the heavy diesel truck, and all three of them stepped onto the porch. They had bed-head, and were wearing shorts and T-shirts. Mason, still in his boxers, not even that much.

"Well will you look at this!" laughed Rogan, pointing to the back of the truck.

I jumped out and proudly flipped the latch that lowered the gate. Our new Christmas tree was lying there on its side, looking fresh and sharp and beautiful.

"You bought a *live* tree?" Desmond asked incredulously.

"I told you I'd take care of it."

"It has a root ball and everything!" said Mason.

"Yup," I confirmed. "We don't even need a stand."

Mason and Rogan jumped up into the truck's bed, and

began sliding the tree out. It came complete with a bright red pail at the bottom, that would allow us to keep it upright.

"I saw this place on our way through town the other day," I explained. "A local guy was selling live trees from his side yard. I figured it would be better than cutting a tree down and killing it for nothing."

"And better than the Charlie Brown Christmas Tree up in the loft," joked Mason.

"Yeah," I laughed. "That too."

Desmond made a face, but I could tell it was just for show. He was smiling by the time he'd helped the others slide the tree out of the truck. Together, they carried it through the doorway and into the cabin.

"The best part," I called after them, "is that you can plant it afterwards. Put it somewhere in your yard. Decorate it every year, to commemorate the best cabin Christmas trip you ever had."

Rogan glanced back over his shoulder at me. "Best we ever had, eh?"

"Shit yeah," I declared, folding my arms happily. "The one trip you were lucky enough to invite *me*."

Nineteen

ALYSSA

It was one of those days that flew by, yet seemed to also last forever. One where you're looking very forward to something specific, but aren't in too much of a hurry to get there, because you're already having the time of your life.

I made my decision around noon, from the top of the mountain. Right before we made our third run, looking out into the crystal blue sky.

I told the guys I wanted to finish the day at the base lodge, and grab a quick dinner there. We'd have a few drinks. Not too many, though, because I still wanted us to decorate the tree tonight.

Then we'd head back to the cabin, where I told them I had a surprise.

The conditions on the mountain were phenomenal all day, and skiing was like floating on a cloud. We rode the lifts and gondolas, laughing and joking. Flirting heavily and without reservation, before stepping off at the icy peaks and gliding effortlessly back down.

Darkness eventually fell, and we retreated to the heat and comfort of the lodge itself. Everything was beautifully-decorated — lit up warmly, with Christmas in mind. We ate light. We drank even lighter. I thought maybe it was because we'd indulged a little too much the previous night. But as two pairs of hands found mine on the way back to the truck, I realized they were just happy to be with me... and maybe just as eager to get home as I was.

Once in the cabin Mason resurrected the fire. Rogan streamed some classical Christmas music, while Desmond untangled three ancient strands of hopelessly knotted twinkle-lights.

I sat cross-legged on the floor, going through box after box of decades-old ornaments. Some were shattered, others were missing hooks. But there was enough to go around. More than enough to make the tree stunningly beautiful, lighting up the living area with all-new warmth and color, as well as an instant holiday feel.

A hand slid over mine, and I realized it was Desmond's.

"Thank you for this," he said genuinely, nodding up at the tree. "And you were right, too. As convenient as it is to put up a fake tree each year, it really *is* more special this way."

I smiled at his handsome, gorgeously-sculpted face. On a whim, I kissed him right on his stubbled cheek.

"Merry Christmas," I told him, very aware of the others watching. "But I should be the one thanking *you* for bringing me here."

In time we finished, then settled back to admire our handiwork. The cabin had been a dark, blank canvas when we arrived. Right now it was breathtakingly beautiful. Mason had the fire roaring, and the twinkling of Christmas lights delivered splashes of color everywhere. We were happy and content. Comfortable. Perfect.

I stood up, and felt the rising anticipation sweep over me right away. My stomach was already doing flip-flops. It was now or never.

"You guys go sit on the couch there," I ordered, "and close your eyes. I'll tell you when you can look again. Maybe a minute or two."

Mason shot me an impish look. "Oh yeah?" he inquired.

"Oh yeah," I confirmed.

Rogan was already seated. Without hesitation, Desmond and Mason both moved to join him. When I was sure they'd hid their eyes, I retreated to my room and shed almost all of my clothing. Then I pulled on my favorite oversized sweater. The really loose, over-the-shoulder one that went all the way down to mid-thigh.

"No peeking, right?" I called after them.

"None," said Desmond.

"Yeah, what he said," Mason grunted.

My legs trembled as I reached the doorway and stopped for a second. This was it. I could still turn back if I wanted. But once I entered that living room...

Oh just do it already!

A half minute later I was lying on my stomach, on the plush carpet beneath the tree. I kicked my legs back and forth in slow, sexy motions, while resting my head in my hands.

"Alright," I said, my voice all but trembling. "You can look now."

All three of them opened at once. And there I was, smiling back at them. Red lips, sparkling green eyes. A bright red, oversized bow that I'd found in the attic... perched perfectly on the swell of my rounded, sweater-covered ass.

"What's this?" asked Desmond. Though I could see in his eyes, he already knew.

"This is your first Christmas present," I said huskily. "Just a few days early."

Rogan and Mason were staring, unabashedly, at every flowing curve of my stretched-out body. Not to mention the big red bow, topping it off.

"And exactly whose present *is* it?" Mason asked carefully.

I took a deep breath and stared pointedly back at them, letting my eyes speak more than any other part of my body ever could.

"Anyone who *wants* it," I purred seductively.

Twenty

ALYSSA

My words were followed by thunderous amounts of silence. And staring. And all *kinds* of other things.

"Alyssa," asked Desmond slowly, "what exactly do you mean?"

"I mean this is what you *want*, isn't it?" Very slowly I scissored my legs back and forth. "This is what you asked me here for?"

Their eyes were locked onto my body. Taking advantage, I pulled up the bottom of my sweater, revealing another inch or two of smooth, naked flesh.

"No," a pair of them said immediately. "I mean, yes," Mason stumbled, "maybe... but was that the *reason* we asked you along with us?" He shook his head. "No. Definitely no."

"We never looked at it that way," Desmond jumped in. "We invited you because we like you. We laugh with you. But this..." he shrugged noncommittally. "This isn't what we wanted."

"Hmm," I said, pursing my painted lips together. "Well... what if it's what *I* wanted?"

My statement knocked them back into collective stunned silence. It was both cute and amusing, as my mouth curled into a wicked smile.

"You did these things with Emma," I said boldly, my pulse picking up speed. "And she *loved* it. I know she loved it, because I read her journal."

They weren't just shocked, they were absolutely astonished. But they were also looking at me much differently now. And that was my goal.

"I'm sorry," I said more to Desmond than the others. "I had insomnia the first night here. I found this book in my nighttable, and... well... I just started to read."

Desmond opened his mouth to say something, but then closed it. There weren't any words, really.

"I was hoping one of you would make a move," I laughed, trying to break the tension. "But—"

"We couldn't," Rogan jumped in. "We sort of, well—"

"We made a pact," said Mason. "An agreement not to hit on you, the whole time we were here."

Now it was my turn to be surprised. "For fuck's sake, why?" I giggled.

"We didn't want it to be awkward for you," said Desmond.

"And we didn't want anyone to be jealous," Rogan added. "If you fell for one of us, the other two would be left out." He stared right through me with those beautiful brown eyes and gave a tiny shrug. "And if you read that journal, you know that none of us have ever been left out before."

In answer, I reached down and pulled the bottom of my sweater all the way up to my waist. The move completely exposed the curve of my ass, which was naked except for the tiniest red G-string.

"Who's leaving anyone out?" I smiled.

The guys were utterly mesmerized now. I felt like I was surrounded by three sexy wolves, all licking their lips.

"You did these things with Emma," I repeated softly. "And now *I* want them. I want to do everything she did. I want to experience the whole thing. All of it. All of *you*."

Holy shit! My heart was hammering out of my chest! I'd jumped off the cliff, so to speak. And now I was falling...

"Are you sure this is really what you want?"

The words came from Desmond. They were low and heavy. Choked with lust.

"Yes," I breathed.

"Because there's no going back," he said thickly. "Once we do this..."

"I know," I smiled. "Trust me. I've been thinking about it the whole time we've been here."

Slowly I rolled onto my back, letting my legs fall apart. I pulled the sweater up just under my breasts, then slid one hand tantalizingly down the flesh of my exposed stomach.

"This is what I want," I murmured, letting my fingers dip beneath the thin fabric of my panties. I worked my middle finger slowly up and down... three, four, five times. Waiting until their eyes were locked on it.

"Alyssa..."

"I want to be your *girlfriend* for the rest of the trip," I said huskily. "All of you. Each of you. I want you to take me *whenever* you want me, anytime, anywhere..."

They were speechless. Totally on edge. But I could feel it in the air — everything had changed. The walls had come down. Their self-imposed restrictions, shattered in the wake of my one wanton admission.

"I want you to take *turns* with me," I whispered nastily, "or go at me together. I want to be pinned between you, just like in the journal."

Slipping my hand from between my legs, I slid that one glistening finger between my lips. Smiling back at them I giggled, holding it between my teeth.

"I want you to use my body like a toy..."

That was it — the last straw. The dam broke, and all three of them left the couch to join me on the floor. Rogan slid down next to the tree, on my right side. Mason took the left. I wondered if they had standard positions, or if they were just winging it, or—

"You know you're in for it," Desmond whispered, kneeling beside my head. He'd bent at the waist. His lips were just inches from mine.

"I know."

He kissed me, deep and slow, holding my head in his lap. I felt four hands moving over me, slowly roaming my body. The feel of a hot mouth, closing over an exposed nipple.

The distinctly promising sound of a zipper...

Oh my God, Alyssa.

Oh my God indeed.

Twenty-One

DESMOND

It was unbelievable, that we were about to do this again. Right here, on this same trip. In the same room, the same place...

Only this time, with the ridiculously hot coworker we'd all been pretty much pursing together.

Then again, why shouldn't I believe it? I'd seen firsthand how much a woman could enjoy what we did. Emma enjoyed it so much she kept it up for three years. She'd even begged for it again and again, as I shared her liberally with my two best friends.

What woman wouldn't keep coming back to something like that? Taking her the way we did, from all sides. Giving her the ride of her life. It was something we'd done to fulfill an exciting fantasy, only Emma and I had *both* found that we enjoyed it way too much to stop.

And now, Alyssa. Lying here in my lap. Reaching into my shorts, and wrapping her delicate hand around my already-swollen thickness...

"Oh wow," she breathed, smiling up at me upside down. "It's *nice.*"

"Sure is." Reaching down ever so gently, I stroked one beautiful cheek. "You know that's going inside you, right?"

Alyssa smiled weakly and nodded back at me. "Sure is."

It was so stupid of me to leave Emma's journal in that nighttable drawer. But in a way, it was lucky too. If I hadn't kept it there, and Alyssa hadn't found it, would we even be where we were right now? Probably not.

Besides, in all honesty I enjoyed it. Every fall I spent a weekend at the cabin, to winterize things and prepare for the snow. Emma usually came with me. We'd go on hikes, and take photos of all the beautiful fall foliage. Only this autumn, I'd been single. This year, I'd come alone.

I found the journal while clearing out some of her things. It was a guilty pleasure — reading about all the things we'd done to her. The loving things. The filthy things. And most interesting of all, reading them from *her* perspective.

God, they'd turned me on all over again.

And now they'd turned someone else on — Alyssa. The beautiful girl I'd been flirting with at the office. The one girl I'd seriously consider dating, after so many months alone.

"Oh my God..."

She was in my lap, stroking me hard. Alternating between kissing me and making out with Rogan, while Mason slid between her beautifully tanned legs and went down on her.

Lucky son of a bitch.

Her green eyes fluttered open, and she looked at me pleadingly. She was lost in lust. One-hundred percent in, on everything we were about to do to her.

It was Emma all over again.

"It feels so... so good..."

I nuzzled my way past her gorgeous mess of auburn hair, until my lips were brushing her ear. The touch made that entire side of her body shudder.

"You know you're in for it," I whispered softly. "Right?"

Alyssa squirmed, gyrating into Mason's mouth. Somewhere between doing that and kissing Rogan, she nodded.

"Because you really *are* going to be our plaything. We're going to *use* you, Alyssa. Every which way." Slowly I traced the outer edge of her ear with the tip of my tongue, causing her to gasp.

"Everything in that journal," I murmured. "That's what you said. Everything that you read about — all those experiences... that's exactly what we're going to give you."

She inhaled sharply, as Mason drove his tongue home. I could see one of her hands, embedded in his hair. Rolling her fingers tight, as her hips surged downward to drive him deeper inside.

"You want to be our *toy*," I teased, throwing her own words back at her. "That's fine. But that also means one thing..."

I tilted her face away from Rogan, and guided the head

of my sex against her full, wet mouth. Our eyes met. Her lips parted.

"For the rest of this trip," I whispered down at her, "your body belongs to *us.*"

Twenty-Two

ALYSSA

They devoured me, head to toe. Kissing me back and forth like there was no tomorrow, then switching places, with my body as their only reference.

It was as dream-like as it was unbelievable: that I was actually *doing* this. That I was giving myself over to three gorgeous men, all eager to take full command over my body. I kept telling myself I barely knew them! And yet, that wasn't true either. It was just something my inner voice screamed as a last warning, perhaps trying to stop me from making a mistake.

But oh... if so, this would be my *favorite* mistake.

The truth was I knew each of them — and I knew them well. Even better now that I was here, hanging out with them. Learning that they were just as fun and funny *out* of the office, as they were dressed in button-down shirts and slacks.

I sucked Desmond deep into my throat, feeling him swell with even more arousal as his strong, masculine hand sifted through my hair. I felt deliciously outnumbered, but not overwhelmed. The center of a slow, relaxed attention, from all three of my soon-to-be new lovers.

Eventually Desmond slid downward, taking Mason's place. I felt his strong arms wrap themselves around my legs. His hands went tight on the insides of my thighs, holding me in place as he took over eating me with that hot, beautiful mouth. I turned my head. Rogan was there, looking down into my half-lidded eyes.

"You're beautiful," he said, and then kissed me. Smiling fiendishly he passed me to Mason, whose lips and chin were glazed with my own tangy juices.

"So hot," breathed Mason. On either side of me, their now naked bodies spooned themselves against mine. "So *sexy...*"

His tongue plunged hotly into my mouth, feeding me a taste of myself. It was so good I could only moan. I was stroking Rogan, getting used to the feel of him. Grabbing Desmond by his wonderfully thick blond hair, and shoving his face even harder against my throbbing crease.

So this is what it's like...

I had a flash of insight. A split-second out-of-body experience, during which I could envision myself from above. Three beautiful men, taking me from three different sides. Three sets of kissable lips. Three hard, pulsating—

Somewhere a switch went off, and I reached the next level. I began stroking the two of them. Pulling them closer so I could alternate licking and sucking on each one. Rogan's shaft was smooth and perfect and beautiful, and fit wonderfully in my mouth. But Mason...

Mason had a really *big* dick.

I gasped the first time I turned to face it, and saw the huge mushroom-shaped head. Lengthwise he wasn't any longer than the others, but that head was enormous.

And he was so. Fucking. *THICK.*

"You've got to be kidding," I murmured, trying to get my mouth around it.

Mason chuckled, lovingly running a thumb over my cheek. "Do your best."

"My best might not be—"

"It will be," he jumped in. "I promise."

Rogan and Desmond switched places, leaving me to focus on Mason. I was licking him top to bottom. Stroking him with my free hand, while running the flat of my tongue all around the girth of his magnificent cock.

This is slutty, Alyssa.

Hell yeah it was. And I didn't even care.

You're going to screw three guys from the office, in the span of the next thirty minutes.

If the realization was supposed to frighten me, it didn't. If anything, the knot of excitement squeezed even tighter in my stomach.

No, I *wanted* this. Wanted it more than anything I'd ever desired before. I'd thought about it. Fantasized about it. And now it was here...

Fuuuuuck...

Rogan's mouth was by far the most talented of the

three. He was doing things to me down there that had my eyes crossing involuntarily. And his fingers—

"Hey..."

I blinked, and suddenly I was staring up into Desmond's eyes. He was smiling placidly.

"You ready for the next step?"

I grabbed the back of his head and kissed him so hard the room started spinning. Everything was warmth and heat and twinkling, sparking lights.

Eventually I nodded dreamily. "And what's the next step?" I asked, though I already knew the answer.

"We carry you into the back bedroom, of course," said Desmond. His mouth slid to my ear, so he could whisper the next line.

"And then we fuck you absolutely *senseless*."

Twenty-Three

ALYSSA

They carried me into the bedroom — literally — with Desmond throwing me over one big shoulder. I was whisked down the hallway. Deposited, with a laugh and a bounce, right onto the surface of the king-sized bed.

But that's where things got serious.

The others took their places on either side of me, while Desmond pushed his way between my legs. I was unbelievably soaked. Sopping wet and ready for anything, as he nudged my thighs apart and guided himself against my throbbing entrance.

I wasn't sure why he got to go first. Maybe because it was his place, his bed. Or maybe he was just the one who took control. Either way it was hot, watching him lean down over my body. Feeling him push the head of his member right up against my folds, before tilting my chin up with two fingers so I could look into his eyes.

"You'll go slow," I laughed nervously. "Take it easy on me, right?"

His expression was unchanged as his sapphire blue eyes blazed into mine. "Slow and easy's going to cost you extra."

I tried to swallow, but couldn't. My throat was tight with arousal I could barely find my voice.

"I'm good for it."

God, he was so *amazing-looking!* His face perfectly-formed, and heartbreakingly handsome. His body, so totally hot and incredibly perfect.

"Slow then," said Desmond, leaning down to kiss me. I felt the electricity as our lips touched. My body rocked downward, beneath his weight. "At first, anyway."

He rolled his hips, and I felt the head go in. Inch by inch he slid inside me, flexing his big arms to keep his massive bulk from crushing my body beneath him.

Oh my Godddd.

The others hung back, and gave us the moment. I could feel the warmth of their bodies against me though. Their lips, nuzzling my shoulder on one side. My neck on the other.

"You're tight," Desmond whispered, his lips barely touching mine. Our eyes were locked. "So very wet though," he murmured. "And so ridiculously *good.*"

My hands slid around his body, settling over his round, muscular ass. He clenched, pushing forward. Shoving himself that final few inches, as my palms felt the powerful muscles coiled just beneath that smooth expanse of hot skin.

Belly to belly, face to face, he kissed me for the first time as full-blown lovers. And then we were *fucking.* His entire length sliding slowly out and then back inside, burying itself deep enough to make me gasp at the end of every beautiful thrust.

My mind went almost totally blank, focusing only on the sheer pleasure of being so well-penetrated and blessedly full. I hadn't been dug out this deeply in ages. Or who was I kidding? Probably ever.

This is sooo worth it.

I tried wrapping my legs around him, but he was just too big. Instead, I let my hands wander. My hands crawled over his magnificent chest, savoring the feeling of it flexing beneath the tips of my fingers. He was drilling me slow but deep. Making my eyes flare wide every time he bottomed out, touching me in places I wasn't sure I was familiar with.

I felt myself sinking into the bed. Enjoying the familiar push-pull of being really, seriously nailed. My last boyfriend, Jonathan, had been sexually regressive. Missionary mostly. Lights off. The kind of lame, placid bullshit that had me pining for my wilder days at Penn State, where I'd had more than my share of interesting sex.

But this...

This was on a whole different level.

Two warm mouths closed over my breasts at the same time, as Rogan and Mason joined in. Already it felt orgasmic.

Holy shit...

My hands left Desmond's ass and went to the backs of their heads, pinning them tightly against my chest. Pulling them hard against me, as I felt them licking and sucking... tracing circles around my areolae. Someone nibbled me, and I jumped. And the whole time, their hands... wandering my body. Getting me hotter and wetter — if such a thing were even possible — as Desmond picked up speed and began plowing the hell out of me.

"What do you want?"

He whispered the question into my ear between strokes. I was so far gone, it barely registered.

"You've read the journal," Desmond murmured. "What do you want us to—"

"Turn me over," I breathed at last.

His face went back to mine, his mouth curling into a smile. As fun as this was for him, I could tell he enjoyed pleasing me even more.

"I want to be spitroasted," I whispered back at him.

I could barely believe I'd said the word. It was in my vocabulary, of course. Between all the boring and terrible sex I'd had while dating Jonathan, I'd watched enough porn that I could probably write and direct my own movies.

Only now I was actually starring in one.

"I want you to—"

My sentence ended in a hard grunt as I was suddenly lifted and flipped onto my stomach. Desmond pulled me backward, to the edge of the bed. He slid to the floor and bent me over the mattress, then re-entered me in a standing position from behind.

Ohhhhhh...

I almost lost it as he pushed himself home, his hands settling sexily into the curve of my hips. He felt even deeper like this. Bigger and faster and—

"Get up on your elbows," he ordered, his breath hot on my ear.

I did what I was told. There wasn't even a question.

"Now pick one of my friends..."

Rogan and Mason were both on the bed, kneeling before me. Stroking themselves toward me with two big, beautiful fists.

Oh my GOD.

I took Rogan first. As amazing as his package was, it was just less intimidating than Mason's.

"That's it..."

My lips parted for him, feeling his hardness as he slid down my throat. At this angle I could take him deep. Leaning on one arm, while gasping him with the other to maximize control.

This is so, so amazing.

I was amazed at how easy it was for the three of us to fall into a familiar rhythm. Desmond behind me, dogging me gloriously deep. Rogan up front, gently pulling my hair back as he guided himself in and out of my mouth. I was pinned tightly between them; the ultimate connection three people could have.

It was just so hot. So unexpectedly intimate...

Nothing's ever felt like this.

The best part was how natural it all felt. Nothing was awkward at all. There was no hesitation, or regret, or shame, or anything that even resembled those things. There was only a strong, steady feeling of elation and happiness. An irrepressible heat and arousal, yes, that too. But also this intangible feeling of *camaraderie* that I didn't expect at all.

I made my lips tight, sucking hard for one last stroke before popping Rogan from my mouth. Then, still bouncing gratefully on Desmond, I looked up for Mason.

But his spot on the bed was empty.

Shit, I thought to myself. *Your first threesome — er, foursome, rather — and you're already leaving somebody out.*

The mystery didn't last long. I felt Desmond withdraw, shift to one side... and then a whole *different* set of hands settled over my hips.

Oh.

My belly went tight. My legs were already trembling.

"Go easy on her man," I heard Desmond chuckle, from somewhere behind me. "She's never done this before."

Twenty-Four

ALYSSA

It was like backing up onto something warm and wonderful... and very, *very* thick.

The thought excited me. Frightened me. Caused my whole body to stiffen, when it needed to relax.

"Easy," said Desmond, holding my face in his hands. "Take your time."

It made me a lot less nervous knowing I was the one in control. That Mason had pledged to stand stock still, and let *me* push back against *him*. Realizing I wasn't about to be abruptly speared made things much easier. Plus, I trusted Mason. Hell, I trusted all of them.

That part seemed strange — maybe even stranger than what I was about to do. I'd gotten close with three people at once. Three very different guys, each of them amazing in their own unique ways.

In that respect it was like any normal relationship: chemistry, attraction, affection, even romance. But it all took place in the three dimensions, on a triple scale.

"Oh my God…"

Mason was inside me now — stretching me pleasantly from within. Another inch. Another moan. Another release of hot breath, through my clenched teeth.

"He's in?"

"No, not yet," Desmond confirmed. "Not all of him."

My eyes widened. "You're kidding?"

"Nope."

"Well… shit."

It felt good, almost too good. But there was also that boundary. That razor thin line between pleasure and pain, that my body was quickly approaching.

Somewhere on the supple flesh of my ass, I felt Mason's fingers flex. He was digging in. Enjoying the feel of me, every bit as much as I was enjoying him.

"Just relax," Desmond smiled. "Go slow… but keep going."

I pictured Emma, going through this herself. Holding her boyfriend's hand, as this very thing happened to her. I imagined how fantastic it would've been, the two of them fulfilling a mutual fantasy. And then afterward, enjoying it over and over again. Year after year…

"That's it. That should be—"

Suddenly I felt it: Mason's body molded against mine. The quivering abdominals of his lower stomach, pressed tightly against the flesh of my ass.

"You okay?"

I closed my eyes. My pussy was squeezing him like it wouldn't let go. In all my life, I'd never felt so wonderfully, blessedly *full*.

"Okay's an understatement," I hissed happily.

"Good," Mason chuckled. "That's what we like to hear."

My newest lover let out a sigh of contentment, then slowly set to work. Screwing him was amazing. My flower clung to him for dear life on the outstroke, but each time he pushed back in it welcomed him home.

Desmond kissed me a few times, softly, tenderly, before stretching his body out before me. In no time I was sucking him. Tasting myself all over his perfect dick, while grinding elatedly back on Mason's impressive thickness.

I could definitely get used to this.

It was heaven, feeling these two powerful men from both ends. Allowing them the pleasure of my willing body, while taking double the amount of pleasure from them. In a flash of insight, I could see how Emma would want to do this again and again. How feeling this loved and attended to could be dangerously addicting, and not just in the physical sense but emotionally as well.

Rogan switched with Desmond, while Mason kept pumping away. He was drilling me with a slow, deep grind that was driving me crazy enough... but then he reached beneath me. I jumped at the pressure of three thick fingers, pressing against the top of my mound.

Oh my GODDDD!

My orgasm was nearly instantaneous. It surged up from my core, washing over me in an explosion of unstoppable heat. Over and over I spasmed, contracting around Mason. Milking his thickness as it stretched me from within, as my eyes screwed shut and my mouth opened and I grunted so loudly it sounded like someone else, not me.

"Hol—Holy Fuuuuuuuck..."

I'd been sliding my tongue all around Rogan, but not now. Right now I was holding onto him for dear life. I dropped face-first to the surface of the bed as I exploded harder than I ever had in my life.

FUCK!

It was shocking — the intensity of it all. I hadn't even realized how close I was. And yet somehow, in the back of my mind, I knew I'd been at the edge the whole time.

Mason was merciful, slowing his movements while I rode out every last ounce of climactic bliss. I could feel him swelling inside me. His shaft thumping and pulsing as he neared his own trigger point, which prompted me to look back over my shoulder and find his eyes with mine.

"Go on," I told him breathlessly. "Do it."

His own eyes were glazed with lust. His expression, far, far away.

"You sure?" he managed.

"Yes," I sighed happily. "Oh *God* yes."

And that was it — the last barrier between us. It dissolved away in an instant, as Mason squeezed and roared and detonated inside me.

"UNNNGGGHH!"

The sound came from his throat, and it was the sexiest noise in the world. Even better that it was accompanied by his spasming manhood, pumping jet after jet of his hot seed somewhere up near my womb.

Oh... oh wow.

He kept ramming me. Filling me. Screwing me through his own violent orgasm, while digging his fingers into my bouncing ass. I'd probably have marks. I didn't care...

"Man, that's so damned *hot*."

I looked back, and Rogan was stroking my face. Pulling my hair back over one ear, so he could gaze into my eyes. I could feel the heat between us. The pent-up chemistry of long months of flirting, about to be unleashed all at once.

"You ready?" I smirked, taking my last parting bounces on Mason. On the last stroke he slid all the way out, leaving me full but empty and wanting more.

"Baby I was *born* ready," laughed Rogan, lifting me in his two beautiful arms and pulling me on top of him.

Twenty-Five

ALYSSA

There were no words, really. Nothing to describe the feeling of riding one incredibly hot man... while kissing and sucking his two best friends.

Rogan was buried so deep it was like he'd become a part of my body. His hands were centered on my hips. He kept lifting his ass from the bed to drive even further inside me, while grinding himself against my ass in slow, delicious circles.

I threw my head back, totally lost in the moment. My mind trying desperately to record every wonderful thing that was happening to my body, so I could play it all back later on. This was the apex of my sex life; the shining pinnacle of my entire erotic existence. I'd never have this again. There wouldn't be anything in my life like it.

Realizing that, I decided to make the absolute most of it.

For a while I took over, bearing my hips down against

Rogan's thrusting pelvis. Grinding my body greedily against his, to elicit every last spark of sensual pleasure being sent to my brain. I clawed at his chest. Grabbed his big, broad shoulders. I cried out toward the ceiling then threw my face downward so I could kiss him while taking him, thrusting my tongue so deep into his perfect mouth it competed with the beautiful erection already buried inside of me.

Eventually his body went rigid, his face contorting into something resembling both pleasure and pain. I laughed out of sheer joy, dropping my face to his. I wanted to watch it happen. To see it in his *eyes* more than anything else.

"Come in me."

With one final, savage thrust he did just that, filling me up from beneath. Rogan's organ pulsed fast and hard, throbbing wildly. I screwed down against him, feeling his balls go tight as they emptied themselves so fully inside me.

"Yes baby, yes..."

My words were low and private – just for us. And the whole time, I kept staring into his eyes. Cementing our physical union with a more intimate connection, before taking his face in my hands and kissing it, softly, over and over again.

I rode Rogan well past the point of being spent and happy, feeling warm and sated and full. Then I slid back into the soft down comforter. I rolled onto my back, smiling up at them as I let my hand wander between my legs.

"You..."

I crooked a finger at Desmond, who still hadn't come yet. It reminded me sharply of what Emma had done from this very same bed, when she invited the second of her new lovers to come forward.

But instead of climbing between my thighs, Desmond only curled his finger back at me. His shaft hung low between his legs, warm and thick and slick with my own sex.

"Let's go."

I sat up and crawled back across the bed, intent on bringing him off. If he wouldn't fuck me, that was fine. There were certainly other ways of making him come.

But the second I got there he scooped me up, sweeping me into his arms.

"OH!"

Desmond held me possessively, supporting my weight easily. The side of my face felt good against his massive chest.

"The rest of the night," he murmured, "you're *mine*."

The others had left the bed, and were already gathering their things. I saw Rogan throw a T-shirt playfully at Mason, who was already stepping into his boxers.

This is old hat for them.

I threw my arms around Desmond, who carried me back into the hall. His own bedroom was cool, almost even cold. But not for long.

"You alright with sleeping with me?"

I whimpered and nodded, nuzzling against his chest. God, he felt so *good*.

A minute later we were beneath the blankets, the cool sheets growing warm against my hot, naked ass. Desmond slid easily between my thighs. He fit perfectly, like he was meant to be there all along.

"We might not get much sleeping done," he warned.

I gasped in pleasure as he sank into me in a single stroke.

"That's okay," I sighed happily. "Sleep's overrated."

Twenty-Six

ALYSSA

"Hey, sleepyhead!" the voice murmured. "Wake up!"

I sat up groggily, rubbing my eyes. I was in a strange room, a strange bed. Sort of.

"Coffee?" I mumbled, before anything else.

"We're not making breakfast today," said Desmond. "We're going out."

He was already dressed, and by the smell of him, already showered as well. Still naked beneath the blankets, I was a total mess.

"Where are we—"

"Vera's kitchen," he replied. "A mile up the road. Best breakfast in all of Vermont."

"O—Okay."

"But we have to hurry," he urged. "She's not going to hold our table forever."

I blinked a few times, then sat up clutching the blankets to my chest. My sudden modestly was almost comical. I wasn't so modest last night.

"I'm gonna need like twenty minutes," I squinted up at him.

"You've got ten."

Nine and a half minutes later I was still wet from the shower, which had thankfully been scalding hot. After soaping up I took it easy on my tired body. Especially the parts that were pleasantly sore.

"I *still* can't believe there's no coffee," I grumbled, ducking into the truck "That's just... wrong."

"You're getting Vera's coffee," Mason smiled from the front seat. "Trust me, you'll be thankful."

Desmond had already lowered the plow, and had everything warmed up and ready to go. He scraped the driveway clean, then plowed whatever fresh snow was still on the road... all the way to what looked like a cute little diner in the middle of the woods.

And the place was absolutely *packed.*

"Do you know Vera?" I asked.

"Uh huh," said Desmond. "Growing up here during the holidays."

"Good thing."

"I did some work on the place too," he admitted. "Helped them add that back extension. Otherwise we'd be waiting ninety minutes for a table."

Sure enough, we were seated straightaway — much to

the chagrin of the two dozen or so waiting patrons. I slid into the tiny corner booth, wondering how the guys would even fit. Somehow they did, but only barely.

It was strange, but so far none of them had mentioned last night. There'd been no conversation about it on the way over. Nothing even hinted about what we'd done.

Are they okay with it?

I knew I was being silly. Of course they were. It occurred to me that maybe *I* was the one being strangely quiet about it.

Well... what exactly do you say in a situation like this?

I really had no idea. All I knew was that the place smelled heavenly; bacon, eggs, fresh biscuits — all good things. And the coffee was everything they'd said it was and more. Totally life-changing.

"Alright," I admitted after the first long sip. "You were right. This was *definitely* worth it."

"See?"

"I mean... wow."

Mason, seated across from me, only winked. "Wow indeed."

A waitress bounded over, and Desmond ordered food for the whole table. It arrived fresh and piping hot, cooked to perfection and seasoned with love. Silence reigned while we devoured everything in front of us, like we'd just wandered in after a week-long trek through the snow. Eventually the guys pushed their plates back, so stuffed they'd even stopped drinking their coffee.

"So how was it?" asked Desmond.

"Fucking amazing," I mumbled, through my last bite of fluffy eggs.

"Not the breakfast," he chuckled. "The sex."

I stopped mid-chew.

"Was it as good as it was in the journal?"

The question was only half honest. I could tell by the sly smiles going around the table, that the guys were challenging me. And I always did love a challenge.

"It was alright," I teased, reaching for another piece of toast.

"Just *alright?*" scoffed Rogan.

"I mean, yeah sure. You guys were great," I smiled. "But you all left so quickly, though."

Rogan and Mason stared back at me open-mouthed, their smiles all but gone. Desmond was still smirking though. He knew exactly what I was doing.

"I kinda figured you'd wear me out," I shrugged. "I mean, there are *three* of you. And there's only one of me..."

Rogan laughed out loud. Mason threw down his napkin.

"Get in the truck," he nodded in the direction of the exit, "and let's head back to the cabin. I'll show you worn out."

Now it was my turn to laugh. "I thought we were going skating today?" I said innocently.

"Skating tonight," Desmond corrected. "Shopping

today."

"*That's* right," I amended with a grin. "You guys promised to take me into town today. Hit some shops. Buy some souvenirs, and—"

"Have lunch," Rogan finished for me.

"Yes."

They were all looking at me now. Probably remembering last night, just as vividly as I was.

"And what if we hit the shops," said Mason, repeating my words, "and then have *you* for lunch?"

My stomach dropped like an elevator, delving somewhere warm and deep. Somehow though, I kept up my game face.

"Well that sounds nice and everything," I said sweetly. "But how will you boys find the energy to go ice skating later if I wear the three of you out?"

Holy shit, who are *you?*

It was a good question. Since last night, it felt almost like a switch had been flipped. Like the words coming out of my mouth weren't my own.

"How about this," Desmond interjected. "Shopping. Lunch. Ice skating..." He paused for a moment to fold his big forearms. "And then straight back to the cabin, where you become dinner."

He was peering directly at me with those big blue eyes. Looking through me, as if staring right into my soul. And that's because Desmond and I shared a secret: he *had* worn me out. He'd taken me back to his bed and screwed me again and again, until the wee hours of the morning, and even beyond. Fucked me until I was so spent and exhausted, I could barely see straight.

"You did say you wanted to be our *toy*, right?"

The butterflies were back. And they'd brought friends this time.

"Yes."

"Well then we're going to play with you all night," said Desmond pointedly. "Over and over again."

I swallowed hard. Eventually, I nodded.

"All *three* of us," added Rogan, stretching his arms theatrically to crack his knuckles. "All over that godforsaken cabin."

Foot, meet mouth.

"Until we wear you *out*," said Mason. His green eyes burned into mine, as his voice went distinctly lower. "We're going to use your body until you beg us to stop."

"*If* I beg you to stop," I somehow corrected him.

You're an asshole Alyssa.

I couldn't help it. My mouth was working overtime, creating a scenario where my body would ultimately pay the bill.

A crazy asshole.

Desmond lifted his arm to call for the check. As he did, the others threw a few bills on the table to cover the tip.

"Better get started then," he said. "We've got a big day."

The Christmas Toy - Krista Wolf

Twenty-Seven

ROGAN

Oddly enough, one of the most attractive things about her was her hair. I loved the way it shimmered. The way it bounced back around her shoulders, every time she flipped it to one side. There was just so much of it, and it felt so damned good between my fingers. Smooth and sleek. Like cornsilk in summer...

Of course, her ass was pretty damned amazing too.

I watched her twist in Mason's arms, turning to face him as she skated effortlessly backwards. Of *course* she could skate. She'd already embarrassed us at skiing. It left us wondering amongst ourselves if she could do practically anything.

And then, last night...

Last night had been totally insane — way crazier than any night had a right to be. Alyssa had shocked us... astonished us. She'd pulled the one card from the deck that had shattered our every perception of her, and utterly voided whatever 'agreement' we'd made between ourselves.

After last night, we didn't have to chase her.

Apparently, she was chasing *us*.

It was shades of Emma. Echoes of our previous relationship. And that's what we'd had, really — a full-blown group romance. What started with Desmond had blossomed into a four-way affair, complete with solo dates and singular connections as well as totally hot, utterly magical, three-on-one sex.

The problem back then was there *was* no problem. Desmond had opened his girlfriend up to being shared by us in every possible way. It went on for months and years — with Mason and I taking Emma whenever and wherever we wanted, almost like she was our own. In many ways, she was. Very quickly, she became every bit our girlfriend as well as Desmond's.

And we all know how *that* turned out.

But now... Alyssa. She was sexy, sassy, fun. Beautiful as hell, and smart as a whip. And apparently — judging from the sounds coming from Desmond's room across the hall last night — totally insatiable, as well.

God, I couldn't stop thinking about her.

It was thrilling, in a way, to finally have her. To take her the way I'd always wanted to, since even before our encounter at work. Alyssa had been on my radar for a long time. Probably too long, because it had taken something like this for me to finally act.

"Hey!"

I looked up and there she was, reaching out for me with one gloved hand. She practically glowed on the ice. Her smile lit up the night.

"You coming?"

I could ski. I could snowboard. But when it came to ice skating...

"C'mon," Alyssa laughed. "I promise I won't let you fall."

My mouth curled into a disbelieving smile. "If I fall, I'm pretty sure you won't be able to stop it. And just so you know, I'm taking you with me."

She grinned back at me and winked. "Then we'll fall together."

The outdoor skating rink was beautiful, all strung out with lights and lit up for Christmas. There was a big tree in the center, topped with a bright shining star. It reminded me of ours, back in the cabin.

"Let's go, speedy," Alyssa teased. I took her hand and let her pull me out on the ice. "Three laps, no falling. Do that, and maybe I'll give you something."

"Something like a reward?" Now she had my attention.

"Exactly like that, yeah."

I thought back to this morning. The three of us had met in the kitchen, before she woke up. We were eager to discuss the previous night's events. Whether or not we'd made a big mistake.

"So we're doing this *again?*" Mason had asked

skeptically.

"No, not again," Desmond was quick to respond. "Nothing like that."

"Then what exactly is it?" I had to ask. "Because let's be honest... it sure *seems* like that."

I watched our friend's face go even more serious than normal. It was always that way, whenever Emma came up in conversation. Slowly, he shook his head.

"Look, this is fun for her," Desmond had told us. "A fantasy she's convinced herself to fulfill. It can be fun for us too, if we're careful with her feelings. Just... don't make it more than it is."

Whatever it was, the whole thing had already happened. That much we couldn't take back. And judging by the size of the smile plastered on Alyssa's face, all day long? It was definitely going to happen again.

"That's it," she said, holding my hand. "Keep those feet facing forward. And don't lock your knees. Skate confident."

"Skate confident?" I chuckled.

"You can get through ninety percent of life strictly on confidence," she said sagely.

I raised an eyebrow. "So what's the other ten percent?"

"Straight up bullshit," she laughed.

Alyssa squeezed my hand and pulled me through the next turn. She was so damned beautiful. And not just in a girl-next-door way, but with a sly seductress vibe layered over top. I loved every curve of her body, from the flare of her hips to her teasing, mischievous smile. She exuded sex, really. On every level.

That's probably because of last night.

Maybe, sure. But I'd wanted her for months now. And after what we'd done in her bed...

"That's three," she said excitedly. "Keep it up, you're almost there!"

We skated the last lap together, enjoying the sights and sounds and scents of our picturesque surroundings. The smell of funnel cakes and cotton candy. Old-fashioned Christmas music being piped in from the overhead speakers. The great mountain lit up above us, each trail filled with skiers. From down here, they looked like tiny ants, crawling through winding tunnels.

Together we crossed past the starting point, and I still hadn't fallen. Alyssa looked rosy-cheeked and radiant. Her smile wider than ever.

"So what do I get?" I asked, sweeping her off to the side of the rink.

She grinned back at me demurely. "What do you want?"

My heart was beating fast now. And it had nothing to do with all the skating.

"I'm not sure I know just yet."

Her arms slid around me. Standing tall on the tips of her skates, she kissed me sweetly.

"Well let me know when you do."

It was a perfect moment. I wanted to freeze it in time.

To put it in my pocket and save it forever, and bring it out whenever I needed it.

"Ahem!"

The sound of Mason clearing his throat turned our attention in a new direction. He and Desmond held out two Styrofoam cups, filled with hot chocolate. As we accepted them gratefully I noticed they'd already returned their skates.

"You guys just about done?"

"Yes," said Alyssa. "I think so."

Desmond rubbed thoughtfully at his goatee. "Back home then?"

We'd surrounded her without knowing it. Created a tiny triangle around her, without even thinking about it.

Just like... well...

"Back home," she smiled brightly, looking at each of us in turn. If she was nervous, it sure didn't seem like it.

Ninety percent confidence.

"To play with toys..." she winked.

Twenty-Eight

ALYSSA

The hot mouth closed over my naked shoulder, giving me shivers as it slid up and down my neck. I was standing spread-eagle in the kitchen. Already stripped down to my cute red bra and matching thong panties, as Mason's hands slid possessively over my body.

"You sure you're ready for this?"

Desmond stood before me, pulling his shirt off. Distracting me with his incredible body. Even so, his question demanded an answer. Lost in my own arousal, I groaned and nodded.

"Because this is your last chance to back out," he warned. "We're ready to take this as far as possible, but before we do, you need to be all in."

I quivered as a hand slipped between my legs. Two eager fingers probed me, easily finding their way past my thong.

"We don't want to lead you down this road," Desmond

went on, "unless you want it. So you have to tell us, Alyssa. You have to—"

"I *want* it," I sighed, reaching back to grab Mason's head. I pulled his mouth harder against me. Felt the heat of his tongue sliding up and down my neck, as his fingers dipped confidently inside me.

My eyelids fluttered. I looked straight back at Desmond.

"I'm the one who read the journal," I told him. "I'm the one who initiated all this, remember?"

Mason's middle finger curled inside me, hitting that one magical spot that made me gasp. I could barely stand up as I melted into his hand.

"You guys have been nothing but gentlemen," I said, "and I gave myself to you, willingly. If anything, it's me pulling the three of *you* down this road."

Another pair of hands slid over my body, as Rogan stepped in as well. He cupped my breasts. Hefted the weight of them in his two warm palms, while Mason's talented fingers kept working inside me.

"If you read the journal," said Desmond, "then you already know about this..."

He held up something sleek and black, with a satin finish. I recognized it immediately, and the area between my legs went that much wetter.

The blindfold.

"I... didn't get to that part yet," I said truthfully. Rogan's mouth closed over my other shoulder, and my eyes closed in esctasy. "I've been... kinda busy..."

"Then what about these?"

I opened again, and found myself staring at a pair of dangling handcuffs. No, scratch that. *Two* pairs of handcuffs.

Desmond's eyes met mine, my stomach did a sexy barrel roll. His expression was deep was arousal... but also, deadly serious.

"Whatever you want," I murmured softly.

His eyes glowed! I mean really, seriously glowed.

"Say that again?"

Mason's fingers were sliding up and down now, through the warm slickness between my legs. He paused at the top, to put an alarmingly delicious pressure on my swollen button.

"I'll do... whatever..." God, I could barely speak! "... you guys... want..." I finished huskily.

Desmond closed the rest of the distance between us, taking my face in his hands. He delivered an open-mouthed kiss filled with such fire, such passion, my legs almost gave out completely.

"That's good," he said, when he was finally finished.

I felt the cold steel of a handcuff sliding over my wrist... followed be a series of slow, ominous clicks.

"That's *perfect*, actually," he whispered hotly into my ear.

Twenty-Nine

ALYSSA

Being the guys' toy, their own sexual plaything... well, it wasn't at all like I expected it would be.

God, it was *so* much better.

They'd taken me down the hall, back to my room — and the scene of the crime. I shouldn't have been surprised when they pushed me face down on the bed. Even less so when they pulled a pair of leather straps from the top corners of the mattress, each with a ring attached to the end.

You've been sleeping on that the whole time, you know.

My heart raced double-time as they blindfolded me, then stretched my arms high overhead. Face down, with my belly sliding against the sheets, they handcuffed me to the rings...

... and then left me there, indefinitely.

In the satin darkness my mind raced, spinning through

a myriad of possibilities of what might happen next. I wished to hell I'd read more of Emma's journal. At the very least I could've skimmed it, to see what happened next.

You know what happens next.

My whole body felt flush with heat. Every nerve ending along my skin tingled, like it was on fire.

Five minutes went by. Ten minutes...

I felt it more than heard it when it happened — the presence of someone else in the room. I was still in my underclothes. Face down, ass up. Positioned totally for *their* pleasure, as Desmond had so succinctly put it.

Someone knelt on the bed, rocking my body backward. A pair of hands went to my ass...

And then all of a sudden a mouth closed over me from behind.

Oh holy shit...

I squirmed slightly against the handcuffs, as a hot, wet tongue went to work on me. I could feel the hands on my ass flexing. Squeezing even more pleasure out of me, as my mystery lover dove head-first into the task of making a meal of me.

He ate me through my thong, virtually inhaling me through the saturated fabric. Then I gasped as he pulled it aside. I felt a hot, wet tongue, driving deep. Licking and sucking and devouring me, as those hands played roughly with my ass to the point where pleasure and pain became barely distinguishable.

I whimpered with joy when he finally penetrated me.

There was another gentle bounce of the bed, and suddenly my lover was pushing inside me from behind.

YESSSS.

I took him easily, greedily, wondering if it could even be Mason. I was really *that* wet. That eager and excited, and maybe even a little pleasantly numb from last night's festivities.

Whoever was screwing me really knew how to fuck, too. They plowed me hard, causing me to sigh with the guilty pleasure of being handled so roughly. They drove achingly deep on every stroke, and added an eye-crossing bump and grind to the end of every thrust, too.

It was so unexpectedly hot, not knowing who it was. Realizing it could be anyone behind me — a stranger, even — which only made the whole thing naughtier and dirtier for me. I trusted them, sure. But at the same time, did I *really* know them?

Don't be stupid, Alyssa.

Maybe in the back of my mind, that was all part of the fantasy. The anonymity of not knowing who was inside me. Feeling safe and protected, yet totally slutty and amazing at the same time.

I humped back against my mystery guest, until I felt the inevitability of his impending climax. His body went tight, his fingers clenched. The distinct changes in his breathing, which by now was almost a series of uncontrollably grunts and groans.

My lover drove forward one last time, and then suddenly and abruptly pulled out. A second or two of confusion later, I felt the unmistakable sensation of hot come shooting across my naked back. Rope after rope of sticky hot seed, raining anonymously down on my skin in some unspeakably hot, ultra-taboo drizzle.

God, I was so close to coming! But somehow I'd missed the window. Instead, I focused on grinding my ass back against my lover's legs. Feeling his rapidly-deflating erection across my lower back and ass, as he rubbed it a few times against the heat of my skin.

A towel landed on my back, abruptly, and then I was being wiped down. Cleaned and prepped for the next person to come through the doorway, whoever that might be.

This is beyond great.

My essence throbbed with need and want, practically begging me to fill it with something again. But like before, I was left alone in the room. Minutes stretched by — minutes that seemed like hours. I was writhing hard against the bedspread. Searching blindly for something — anything at all — I could wedge between my legs, to maybe get off on and relieve some of the pent-up, pre-orgasmic tension building up in my lower body.

And then it would happen again... and again after that. The creak of a floorboard. The spidery hint of a breeze, as someone else stepped into the room.

I was devoured from beneath. Eaten again, from behind. I had my breasts kissed and licked and nuzzled, while being fingered into a frenzy. I had someone pressed tightly against my lips, just beneath the fabric of my blindfold.

And each time, I was screwed hard afterward. My thong pulled tightly to the left and right, stretched high over one asscheek as I was entered roughly from behind. It was amazing, doing all of this blind. Not even having the benefit of my hands to identify which of the hard, muscular bodies currently ravaging me belonged to whom.

One or two of them left without even coming. They screwed me until they couldn't take it anymore, or until I was just on the verge of my own feverish orgasm. Then they'd just stop... and walk away.

God!

It was the most frustrating thing in the world, to be left on the quivering edge of my own climax. Yet in some ways, it was also strangely amazing. There was an undeniable thrill involved with not knowing *anything* about what came next. A blind excitement that came with knowing I was there to please *them*, and that they were using my body for their own personal gratification.

I was ravaged again and again, until someone else came on my ass with a long, savage hiss. I could feel their balls, swelling against my back as they rode out their orgasm. The heat of their sizzling ejaculate, dripping down the backs of my thighs...

Fuck!

I don't know how long I lay there. I lost track of how many times they went. One man left. Another man entered. Over and over strange hands went to my hips, and I never knew whether I'd be devoured or dogged or a combination of both. I was getting *desperate* to come. Totally consumed with the need for release, to the point where I began thrashing and crying out. I was bucking backwards against anyone inside me, and even *begging* out loud, to be permitted to come.

Whoever it was who took mercy on me, I would've

married them on the spot. My last lover continued thrusting past the point where the others had quit, right as my wrists began twisting in the handcuffs. My body went rigid. My hands wrung the air in desperation, as I prepared for the worst...

Only the worst never happened.

Ohhhhh... YES!

I came and came again, all over the blessedly thick erection still buried inside me. The warm body behind me didn't withdraw. The hands on my hips remained tight, the monster inside me kept thrusting away, hammering itself home, stroking me from the inside out, all through the glory of my orgasm.

I might've even blacked out. With the blindfold on, it was impossible to say. All I remember is lying limply on my belly. And then a voice in my ear, whispered so low and raspy I couldn't tell who it was.

"Are you hungry?"

I nodded weakly. I was famished, actually. It had been so many hours since lunch, it may as well have been—

Ohhh!

My thoughts were interrupted as a mushroom-shaped head was pushed abruptly past my lips. And then suddenly my lover was coming — pulse after pulse of thick seed, warm and heavy, filling my mouth in an instant.

Oh...

I opened wide, wanting it all. Eager to make this man feel even half as good as he'd just made me feel, by bringing him off as fully as possible in my churning, swirling mouth.

He fed me for what seemed like forever, holding my head in place. Eliciting low, primal grunts, as he blasted the second half of his climax straight down my throat.

It was thick. Sweet. Musky. All at once. And oh so very, *very* hot.

"There..."

I still couldn't identify the voice. It could've been any of them. Or it could've been all of them, standing around me. Watching. Waiting their turn...

"Are you *still* hungry?"

I swallowed one last time. Hesitantly, I nodded again.

"Good."

I felt tension on my arm. The metallic click of a lock, and the abrupt freedom of one of the handcuffs letting go.

"Get yourself together," the voice said, as a key was pressed into my palm. "Dinner's just about ready."

Thirty

ALYSSA

I wasn't sure what was more exciting, really. That I'd been chained to my bed and used like a toy, or that the guys had taken turns tag-teaming dinner... while taking turns tag-teaming me.

"Salt, please?"

I slid the little plastic container Mason's way, and he proceeded to dump it all over his french fries. Dinner was simple: cheeseburgers and hot dogs, cooked on the grill out back. The guys must've spent half the time shoveling out the patio, that's how covered everything was back there. I knew all too well how they spent the other half.

"So are we still doing ice-fishing?" asked Rogan, mid-bite.

"Maybe," said Desmond. He smiled and pointed a fry my way. "Depends on our girl here."

The others regarded me skeptically. "She doesn't look like a fisherman," said Mason. "Err... fisherwoman."

It was great how casual everything suddenly was. We were eating dinner, talking about what we wanted to do during our vacation. As if they hadn't just taken turns screwing me silly, only minutes earlier.

"Do I have to outfish you the same way I outskied you?" I challenged.

"Can you?"

I let out a mischievous laugh. "Maybe."

"What kind of—"

"Striped bass, mostly. Bluefish too." I started counting on my fingers for effect. "Porgies, fluke, flounder..."

Mason grunted. "Oh boy."

"Blackfish, weakfish—"

"Okay, okay," Desmond laughed. "We get it. Somehow or another... you can fish."

"Well I *am* a Jersey girl," I shrugged. "My uncle owned a boat, and rented a shore house every year. He took us out a lot."

"What about that snowshoe tour?" Mason asked.

Rogan shook his head. "That sounds exhausting."

"Ice climbing?"

"That sounds dangerous," I said nervously.

"It's not so bad, actually," Mason countered. "Bingham falls has a level one waterfall."

"What the *hell* is a level one waterfall?" asked Rogan, screwing the cap off his latest beer.

"Hell if I know," laughed Mason. "Saw it online, though."

I crossed to the fridge and pulled out another beer of my own. Mind-blowing sex aside, I really loved being here. I was feeling comfortable. Cozy. And best of all, I finally had someone to spend the holiday with. Or rather, someones.

"Whatever we decide to do," said Desmond, "it's gonna have to happen over the next day or so. Storm's coming. A big one."

We'd heard it on the radio, on the way back from town. A blizzard was coming, right up the middle of the state.

"We're probably getting snowed in for Christmas," Desmond added.

"Well we'd better go shopping again then," I declared. "I haven't gotten you boys *anything*."

They fell silent as a trio, each of them looking back at me over their food and drink. Each with his own knowing smile.

"Oh I don't know about *that*," joked Rogan.

"Besides that," I said, sticking my tongue out at him.

The idea had appealed to me since before I'd even gotten here: getting snowed in with my three gorgeous coworkers. Trapped in our cozy little cabin, with nothing to do but—

"Fuck."

We all turned to face Rogan.

"What?"

"I just realized, I didn't ship out my niece's birthday gift."

Mason whistled. Desmond muttered something unintelligible.

"When's her birthday?" I asked.

"Tomorrow."

"That sucks," I declared.

"I know, I know," bemoaned Rogan. "Don't rub it in."

"No, I mean it sucks that her birthday is so close to Christmas. Every year it gets lost in the shuffle." I thought for a moment. "How old is she?"

"Ten."

I stood up abruptly and extended my hand. "Come with me."

It was a simple thing, to plod down the hall and back into the master bedroom. The handcuffs were still on the bed. I swept them to one side and pulled out my laptop.

"What's she like?" I asked.

Rogan shrugged. "Well, she's about four-foot nothing. Blonde hair. Blue eyes—"

"I mean what *does* she like?" I grumbled begrudgingly.

"Oh," Rogan laughed. "Uh... well, she likes to draw. And make things. And she likes science stuff."

"So she's creative."

"Yeah. Definitely."

Ten minutes later I had a shopping cart filled with everything a creative little girl could want. Color cord bracelets. Stencils. A glow-in-the-dark terrarium that I would've clawed someone's eyes out for, had they had such a thing when I was a little girl. Even an origami butterfly kit.

"There," I said, satisfied. "And because you're such a good uncle, you'll be springing for next-day shipping."

I clicked. Rogan winced.

"Oh don't be like *that*," I laughed. "It's your fault you were late to this party. Now... what about Christmas?"

"I do Christmas with my sisters after the new year," he said.

"Sisters?"

"Yup, three of them."

"How come?"

"Because they're on the panhandle and it's a pain in the ass," he smiled.

"Your family should never be considered a pain in the ass," I scolded him.

"Oh yeah? And what about yours?"

I opened my mouth to reply, then stopped abruptly. He had me there.

"How come you never spend Christmas with your parents?" asked Rogan. "Or at least your sister. I know she lives out in California. It's beautiful on that coast."

"My parents..." I found myself struggling. "Well, they're kind of a lost cause. And my sister's an entirely different person now. She and I don't relate anymore."

"But you relate with us?" said Rogan, pulling me to his side of the bed.

He was one of those people who could smile with his eyes. His expression was warm. Non-judgmental.

"You guys are different," I said.

He turned me gently onto my back. Positioned himself over me.

"We are, huh?"

I bit my lip and nodded.

"In all good ways, I hope?" he said, his lips drawing ever closer to mine.

His lips brushed mine, sending tingles up and down my body. He wasn't kissing me though. Not yet. Just touching lips. Breathing my own hot breath, while staring deep into my eyes.

"I know what I want now," Rogan whispered into my mouth. "For my ice skating reward."

His hand slid up my leg, to rest tantalizingly at the junction between my thighs. He pressed inward, firmly but gently, cupping my sex. I let out a whimper as he gave me a gentle squeeze.

"You do, huh?"

"Yes."

I tried grinding upward into his hand, but he pulled back just enough to thwart me. As I lowered my ass back to the bed, he pushed forward again, teasingly.

"What then?"

I envisioned him rolling my yoga pants down my legs, right there on the bed. Sliding between my thighs and tunneling into me straight away, while the others cleaned up dinner.

Instead, Rogan planted a single kiss on my lips. Then he bounced up from the bed and left my lying there, all hot and breathless.

"I'll show you later," he winked, before leaving the room.

Thirty-One

ALYSSA

Oh what a difference a year makes!

It's still unbelievable to me, that it's really been that long. That we were back here all over again, in the place where it all began. I'd wanted to keep a journal all year, but there was just too much to talk about. Too many amazing things we'd done when we got back to Florida... the four of us, together.

I knew from the start it might end up like that. That once the genie was out of the bottle, that was it. Desmond agreed; there was no reason to stop.

Not that I could stop if I wanted to, at this point.

There were times during the year when we slowed down, especially as we all got busy. But then there were the other *times. The times when one or more of them would go crazy on me... or more often than not, me on them.*

Twelve months since last Christmas. Twelve crazy months of me being shared between my boyfriend and his two hot friends. I didn't keep a journal like this one, but I did keep a list. A list of experiences I'm jotting down below, for posterity and future reference.

Not that there's a chance in hell I'd ever forget them...

My pulse was already racing as I flipped the page, ready to read about Emma's year. I needed to know what happened after the cabin. How things had gone between the four of them, once their holiday was over and the reality of being home in Florida had set in.

Apparently, their little fantasy had carried over. Because the four of them had done all *kinds* of amazing things:

THINGS I REMEMBER:

~ The very first time we all got together at my apartment, once we got back. Desmond invited the others over for drinks, knowing full well what he had in mind. Rogan and Mason sat around awkwardly, looking adorably cute and hesitant. At least until I paraded out of the bedroom in all-new lingerie.

~ The first time I had the boys over to my place for dinner. And how totally hot it was, doing all three of

them in my own bed.

~ Rogan's birthday, and me being designated as his present. Desmond dropped me at his place after work, to surprise him in nothing but a G-string and a trenchcoat. I'll never forget the look on his face as he opened the door! And how funny it was, with him texting Desmond to make sure everything was okay… while I was already busy going down on him.

~ The fourth of July, at the beach, watching fireworks. Lying between the three of them in the darkness. Being kissed by them over and over, until I was dizzy. And how amazing it felt being screwed deep into the sand, on our fuzzy blanket, while the three of them took turns keeping watch.

~ The night Desmond 'lent' me to Mason to repay a football bet, that I'm pretty sure they didn't even make.

~ The time Mason and I went out for a beer run, and ended up screwing our brains out in the back seat of his car.

~ The night of my birthday. Going out to dinner with Desmond, and then back to a fancy hotel downtown… where Rogan and Mason were already waiting in nothing but their boxers.

~ Halloween, and going out on a trick-or-treating bar crawl with all three of the guys. Dressing up like a slutty nurse. Going back to Mason's place because it was closest, and then playing 'doctor' on them until I'd

made them all come inside me.

The list went on and on. There were almost two-dozen instances of Emma's sexual exploits, each hotter than the last. And despite being so well taken care of today, each one making me *that* much wetter.

My favorite however, took place when Desmond had traveled overseas on a business trip, two summers ago.

I could actually remember him being away from the office, when I thought about it. For the three weeks he was gone, Emma had apparently been dubbed Rogan and Mason's official girlfriend. The title came with every conceivable sexual perk, as the two of them took turns watching over her, which of course meant sharing her bed.

And sometimes they'd even shared that bed together.

I wanted to keep skimming the journal, but it was already late. It was cold and dark and well past midnight, and the guys — having apparently worn *themselves* out on me this time — had already turned in.

I clicked off my reading lamp, and slid the nighttable drawer open. Halfway to putting the journal away, I noticed someone standing in my doorway.

Rogan.

"You wanna keep reading about that stuff?" he asked coyly. "Or would rather be *doing* it?"

I closed the drawer without taking my eyes off him. He was intentionally shirtless. The delectable peaks and valleys of his six-pack abs, all ripped and amazing.

"What did you have in mind?"

"Well my bed's warm," he said, shifting from one foot to the other. The muscles of his stomach danced in waves. "Much warmer than in here."

"So... a sleepover?"

He let out a roguish chuckle. "Yeah. Something like that."

I went to throw back my covers, then hesitated.

"Shouldn't I ask my parents?" I teased.

"Nah. I think not."

"Why?"

"Because you're probably going to be doing some very naughty things."

I raised an inquisitive eyebrow. *"Probably?"*

Rogan stepped forward and yanked the comforter off my body so fast I yelped. I bounced down, covered in goosebumps, as he slid both hands around to cup my ass.

"Get in my bed and find out," he growled sexily.

Thirty-Two

ALYSSA

It was the best Christmas Eve I'd ever had.

We spent our last hours before the storm running around town. Milk, eggs, bottled water — these things were already scarce by now, but somehow Desmond knew exactly where to get them. He'd spent too many winters here. He knew too many people. They saved things for him, and I saw him kiss enough women on the cheek and shake enough men's hands to realize he was well-loved.

Each of us peeled off in different directions to do some shopping of our own. Everything closed down early, though. Everyone was getting to wherever they had to go, before the blizzard pretty much kept you locked inside wherever you happened to end up.

And I wanted nothing more than to end up in the cabin with my three beautiful boys.

As good as yesterday had been, last night was like a dream come true. Rogan had taken me back to his bed as promised, and there I found Mason still up and waiting for me. I'd climbed happily between the two of them. Enjoyed the warmth of their broad bodies pressed snugly on either side of me...

And then they'd taken turns kissing and making out with me for what had to be a whole *hour.*

It was insane, how turned on I could get from *just* kissing. The gentle feel of a slow probing tongue. The swoon of passion that came with breathing someone's every breath.

Together they made up for every single kiss I'd missed out on, while being chained to my bed. That had been pure sex. Raw, animalistic. But last night...

Last night was *intimacy.* A total emotional connection, on every level. Rogan and Mason had kissed and nuzzled and cuddled me, until I was dripping and squirming between them. And then they'd made love to me, one by one. First Mason, pushing his way between my legs... and then Rogan, taking his place right away, as soon as his friend had spent himself inside me.

They'd kissed me throughout, rocking me gently on my back. Bringing me off not once but *twice*, as I wrapped my arms around them and spread my thighs as wide as they could go. And it all happened beneath the covers. They'd screwed me slowly, leisurely, without ever breaking the seal of the comforter and exposing my naked skin to the cool, cabin air.

Whether Desmond knew or not, he didn't show it in the morning. And then I realized it didn't matter. The three of them had an unspoken agreement that now included me. I was served nothing but coffee and smiles. Nothing but love and caring and a deep, unrelenting respect.

I could get used to this.

It put a pang of excitement in the pit of my stomach. The idea that something like this could go on and on, even beyond going home to Florida.

They did it with Emma... why not me?

I spent the entire afternoon pondering that exact question. Ransacking shop after adorable shop for trinkets and tchotchkes and the occasional gift, while daring to believe what we had on our little holiday trip might blossom into a recurring thing.

But was that what I really wanted?

It seemed totally crazy, when I thought about it. Living out the fantasy between the four walls of our little cabin was one thing. In that respect our romance was just like our vacation; it had a beginning and an end. The whole thing was finite, and maybe that made it more acceptable in my head. That I wasn't *really* doing these things, simply because I wouldn't be doing them for any significant length of time.

Unless...

I was in my room wrapping presents when I heard a knock at the door. Desmond walked in, looking big and beautiful and amazing. Even in his thick winter coat.

"I've got a quick errand to run," he said, one hand still on the doorknob. "Want to come with?"

"An *errand?*" I said, shocked. "Now?"

"Yeah."

"But the storm's about to start!"

"All the more reason we need to get going."

I swung my legs over the bed, and started looking for my boots. Desmond was already holding them up.

"What kind of—"

"Mr. Foster is snowed in about a half mile from here," he explained. "We're gonna plow him out. Then we're gonna give him a ride to his family in Morristown, so he's not trapped alone in his house for Christmas."

I envisioned the whole thing. My heart melted.

"That's about the sweetest thing I've ever heard," I said.

"Yeah," Desmond smiled handsomely. "We're gonna be heroes..." He glanced out the window behind me. "But only if we hurry."

Thirty-Three

DESMOND

The storm was coming on faster than I expected. Still, I wasn't worried. There was something comforting about having Alyssa beside me in the cab of the truck.

"It's gonna come down heavy, isn't it?" she asked.

"Yeah. Big and fast."

She chuckled from her seat. "Exactly how I like it."

I pretended to roll my eyes as she elbowed me playfully. It was so much fun, having her here. Somehow she fit in perfectly among three alpha guys, and not just in the physical sense.

It's because she's smart. Funny. Laid back.

Yeah, Alyssa was definitely all those things and more. She was self-effacing, and rolled with the punches. Like us, she didn't take herself too seriously.

And that was a rare thing nowadays.

Our task was done, and we were now on our way back

to the cabin. Mr. Foster had been grateful. The drop-off had gone smoothly.

"How many feet you think we'll get?"

"Could be as much as five or six," I replied, eliciting a low whistle from Alyssa's side of the cab. "Or so I heard."

If anyone knew how the snowstorm would go, it was the two of us. Rogan and Mason were Floridians through and through. But I'd spent winters here, and Alyssa was a Jersey girl. She'd seen her fair share of snowstorms and blizzards, even if they were on a smaller scale.

"Go slower," she said abruptly.

I looked over to where she was staring out the passenger window and into the darkness.

"Trust me," I explained. "There might not be many streetlights up here—"

"Or any streetlights up here," she interjected.

"—but I can totally handle the road," I finished.

She was smiling now, but not at what I'd said. It was more a sly, devilish smile.

"Oh I trust you," she said matter-of-factly. "But that's not why I told you to slow down."

I opened my mouth, but before I could get a word out she slid over and dropped a hand on my upper thigh. Her eyes flashed as she gave me a not-so-gentle squeeze. Then, wordlessly, she began fumbling with the button on my jeans.

"I— uh... Oh."

She laughed. "Oh? That's all you have to say?"

My zipper came down. A warm hand wormed its way into my boxers.

"I... well..."

"You don't have to say anything, really," she said mercifully. Leaning closer, she put her lips right up against my ear. "All you have to do is lift your ass from the seat," she whispered, "so I can slide your pants down to your knees and *suck you off...*"

The wicked emphasis she put on those last three words sent a spark of electricity through my body. I felt myself stiffen, straining against her roving hand.

"The trick to road head," she giggled, "is to drive slow and keep your eyes on the road. Otherwise... well..."

She dropped her head into my lap, pulling me manhood free. It was thick and sleepy, but rapidly waking up. Especially as she put her lips against the shaft and planted a kiss there.

"Of course, this is all in theory," she said. "I've actually never *given* road head."

I jumped as a hot, wet tongue slid its way up my length. My foot gunned the gas pedal in reflex, and the engine revved temporarily. I heard her laugh into my lap.

"Have you ever received road head?" she asked.

I shook my head, then realized she couldn't see the motion. "No," I finally said. "Never."

"Good," Alyssa murmured. "Then we'll both lose our road virginity to each other."

Her mouth closed over me, sending me straight to

heaven. Her tongue swirled sexily, just beneath the head of my now-hard erection. I could feel the softness of her hair, brushing against my stomach.

Ohhh, that feels so good...

It was just like she said it would be — a total distraction. I had to pry my eyes away from her beautiful bobbing head, to look back on the road. The snow was falling now, in thick heavy flakes. I could see them passing through the beams of the truck's big headlamps, as I rolled slowly down the deserted road.

This is crazy.

The voice in my head could've been referencing the molten hot blowjob I was getting right now. But it just as easily could've been referring to our overall situation. Somehow, we were doing it again. Rogan, Mason and I, sharing the same woman. Doing the same incredible things to her... while falling deeper into the inevitable attachments of last time.

At first I'd convinced myself that it would just be sex. That we were doing nothing more than fulfilling a coworker's fantasy, brought to us by *her*. After all, Alyssa had initiated everything. As far as I knew, we'd been true to our agreement and steered clear of going after her.

And then she'd come to *us*.

I sighed with happiness, as she added another hand to the mix. Alyssa was sucking me off as I drove us home. Pumping the base with one hand, while using the other to gently roll my balls between her nimble fingers.

My hands gripped the steering wheel so hard I thought

I could tear it right off. It felt that. Fucking. Good.

Go slow, remember?

I eased off the gas some more, though I was already rolling slow. I wanted to enjoy this. To savor the feel of her churning, swirling mouth, engulfing me lovingly, as the heat from the truck's vents washed over my face.

I thought about what we were doing, and how similar it was to... well... Emma. Shit, it was damn near identical. And yet, it was also wholly different as well.

Emma had started as my girlfriend, as well as being the boss's daughter. That had complicated things, even as the four of us struggled to keep things simple. With Alyssa however, we'd all started at once. It was a level playing field. No real history but the history we were making right now.

And what happens next?

It was something the guys had both taken me aside and asked me in private. But even before that, it was a question I'd asked myself. Would we all keep going, even after we got home from the holiday? Or would it be smarter to just end things when our plane touches back down in Florida, and go back to the professional relationships we had before?

Even more importantly... what would she want?

I had no idea, really. All I knew was that the girl between my legs was everything I ever wanted in a woman. She was intelligent, witty, and cool. Breathtakingly gorgeous. And she could hang with my two best friends, obviously.

And although it was technically my first time, I could already tell she gave the best road head in the world.

"Baby..." I all but gasped. "Baby I'm gonna—"

"Mmm-hmm."

One hand left the wheel involuntarily, my fingers sifting through the silk of her hair as my orgasm rapidly approached. Alyssa relaxed her grip on me, but tightened the seal of her lips. Everything between my legs felt warm. Wet. Wonderful.

"Oh my God..."

I erupted violently, filling her mouth with my cream, feeding her everything that I had. My balls boiled over as pulse after pulse of searing hot ecstasy rushed out of me.

Fuuuuck!

I felt it go past her talented mouth. Straight down her throat, and into her belly. Alyssa took it all without stopping, without ever taking her mouth from my surging, pulsing shaft. She swallowed every last drop while pumping me gently, until I was drained and weak and floating on a beautiful cloud of dopamine.

"Holy shit, Alyssa..."

She smacked her lips as she sat back up, and those lips were plump and full. She looked more beautiful than ever, her face all flush with heat. Her eyes shining in the dashboard lights, like liquid fire.

Staring at her beautiful face, a wave of intense feelings crashed over me. Feelings that were abrupt, yet familiar. Feelings that tightened the knot in my stomach.

"That was a whole lot easier than I thought it would be," she chuckled.

The Christmas Toy - Krista Wolf

Thirty-Four

ALYSSA

"Go on," Mason smiled. "Open it."

I knelt beneath the tree, holding the third of my four gifts. This one was wrapped in silver and blue paper, with a beautiful red ribbon.

"Can I shake it?"

Mason's eyes narrowed. The others laughed.

"What?"

"Actually you're *supposed* to shake it," smiled Rogan. Almost immediately, Mason shot him a dirty look.

"I *am?*"

I shook the package, which was small but heavy. I expected some kind of result, but it made no sound.

"Alright," Desmond laughed. "Let's end the suspense already."

I pulled on the ribbon, and found a box within a box.

Inside that, my hand closed over something round and smooth and cold. When I pulled it out, I was holding the most beautiful snow-globe.

"Oh my God," I breathed. "It's *gorgeous!*"

It really was. This wasn't some ordinary run-of-the-mill globe, it was an expensive, detailed replica of the town we were in. I could see the tiny shops of main street, all colorfully painted. The pure white spire of the Stowe community church, rising above all else.

"Do you like it?" Mason asked hesitantly.

I shook it again, and tiny flecks of glittery snow swirled through the little town. It created a perfect storm that matched the one still raging outside.

"Like it?" I jumped up from where I was squatting on the floor and leapt into his lap. "I *love* it!"

Mason's arms went around me as I kissed him square on the mouth. What began as a sweet thank you kiss turned a lot less innocent, as our lips churned and our jaws rotated and our tongues touched.

"Easy now," Desmond admonished. "Let's not fall into that trap again," he chuckled. Then, with a sideways glance at the others: "Yet."

I extracted myself from Mason's two strong arms, and eventually went back to the tree. The guys had already finished unwrapping their gifts. They'd opened each other's "not-so-secret Santa" presents, which I learned comprised of them standing in a circle on Thanksgiving and each buying a gift for the person to the right. All of them were gag gifts, of course. And all three were hilarious.

My last-minute gifts to them were slightly less resourceful, but just as funny. Rogan got a keychain inscribed with *I LOVE FUCKING YOU,* and beneath that, *I MEAN I FUCKING LOVE YOU.* I gave Desmond an oversized coffee mug that said *THANKS FOR ALL THE ORGASMS,* and Mason got a stainless steel bottle-opener that said *I LOVE YOU FOR WHO YOU ARE, BUT THAT DICK SURE IS A BONUS.*

Along with those, I gave each of them a heartfelt, hand-written card thanking them for such a beautiful Christmas. Of course, I couldn't stop there. Inside each card was a coupon granting the bearer one free hour of ANYTHING he wanted. Sexually, of course.

"But you're already our toy," Mason had pointed out. "You're already doing whatever we want."

"Maybe so," Rogan had replied, holding up his own coupon. "But these things don't have expiration dates."

Whether intentional or not, I'd left the coupons suspiciously open ended. Which could only mean one thing...

You're asking for it in Florida, too.

I swallowed dryly at the realization. The thing making my throat even more tight however, is that *they* were realizing it too.

"Alyssa," Desmond called out, snapping me back to the present. "Go ahead and open your last present."

My fourth gift – the special one – was from all three of them. I couldn't possibly imagine what it was.

"I feel bad," I said, lowering my head.

"What the hell for?"

"Because you guys got me such thoughtful things," I said, staring down at the small, rectangular-shaped box. "And I... well... all I got you were gag gifts."

"But we *love* our gag gifts," said Desmond, hefting his mug.

"I know, but—"

"Look, we all shopped last minute," interrupted Mason. "And half the stores were souvenir shops."

"Still..."

Rogan left his chair by the fire, climbing onto the floor beside me. He tilted my chin upward with a gentle touch.

"Listen, this last gift isn't really that thoughtful," he said with a roguish smile.

I let out a short laugh. "Promise?"

"Oh yeah," said Mason.

"Totally not your standard Christmas gift," Desmond agreed.

"Alright then," I chuckled, tearing into the package. "This had better not be anything good."

I hadn't been this happy for the holiday in years. I was thrilled and excited, like an actual kid on Christmas morning.

"Oh we didn't say it wasn't good," warned Rogan.

"Yeah," Mason agreed. "Just that's it's not gonna be... well..."

I opened a box within a box, and I was left staring at a strange, smoothly-curved object. It was a bright hot pink. Wide at one end, and narrow at the other.

"This is a sex toy, isn't it?"

I glanced up at Mason, who only looked away. Rogan whistled merrily.

"Thought so," I giggled.

"Ah, but it's not just any sex toy," said Desmond. "Pick it up."

I took it from the package, turning it over a few times in my hand. It was small, but I could see where it went. Or rather, where it was *supposed* to go.

"That," Desmond continued triumphantly, "is the Lovense Lush."

I gasped as the thing jumped alive in my hand, vibrating and pulsating against my palm. There were no switches to hit. No buttons to press. Yet somehow...

"What did you—"

I looked again, and Desmond was holding nothing more than his phone. He had an app open, with two parallel bars on it.

"We're going to have a lot of fun with this," he said, sliding one finger along the bar. The curved, vaguely egg-shaped object buzzed even harder in my hand.

"Especially *you*," he winked.

Thirty-Five

ALYSSA

"I love you..."

The words hung there for a moment, traversing nearly three thousand miles in the span of an instant. The resulting silence was uncomfortable. And then:

"I–I love you too."

I hung up the phone feeling emotionally drained. But also, charged up. Somewhat... accomplished.

"So you did it, huh?"

Mason stood leaning against the counter, drinking milk directly from the carton. I would've admonished him, but he finished the container and threw it out.

"Yeah. I did it."

"And what'd your sister say?"

"The usual," I sighed. "California stuff."

Kate and I had spent about six whole minutes on the

phone. Five of them were occupied by her talking about herself. But that was typical, and I was used to it.

What I wasn't used to, was saying 'I love you'.

"And your parents?" asked Mason.

"I called them too," I replied. "Mom's good. Dad's hip is acting up. They're in Ramsey right now, staying with friends."

"Well good," he replied, folding his arms. "We might all have disjointed families, but we're not barbarians. It's the one rule we have around here: we call our families for Christmas, whether they like it or not."

"I thought your one rule was that I was off limits?" I smirked.

"You *were* off limits," Mason shot back. "But now?" He smiled evilly. "It's open season on your ass."

My ass, huh? I almost said but didn't. Still, it was cute. That these three big macho guys all went soft enough to call their mothers for the holidays. Or in Mason's case, his father.

"How'd it go with your dad?" I asked.

He hesitated for an awkward moment. "Not bad."

"But not good either?"

I knew from the others that Mason's mother had passed. His father had moved on and remarried rather quickly, and Mason probably resented him for it. From what Desmond told me, he had a whole new family now. A pair of stepsons from his new wife's previous marriage, as well as two daughters of their own.

"So what about your sisters?" I asked, when he hadn't answered.

"They're not really my sisters."

"They're your *half* sisters," I told him, a little shocked at how cavalier he was being about all this. "Sorry, but that's family. They're your *sisters*. Your blood."

"Yeah well..." he hesitated again. "I don't think my dad wants me to have a relationship with—"

"How old are they?"

He paused for a moment to do the math. "Ten and twelve."

"Holy shit, Mason! That's old enough to be hanging out with." I shook my head. "You could have a whole relationship with them, regardless of your interaction with your father. You could be the cool-as-hell big brother."

"They already have two big brothers," he said simply. "They don't need me."

"You should be taking them to the mall," I said dismissively. "Or the movies. Or anywhere, really. Mason, you should be doing stuff together. Having fun with them."

My lover shifted uncomfortably on the other side of the kitchen. He still wasn't sold. Or maybe he just wasn't interested in buying at all.

"Calling your dad once or twice a year doesn't accomplish anything," I said, crossing the kitchen. "Except maybe to assuage your guilt, or—"

He reached out when I got near enough, and pulled me close. Hip to hip, face to face, I could feel the warmth of his body against mine.

"What's the good of having a family if you're not willing to spend time with them?" I asked softly.

Our eyes locked, and I could see the emotions playing inside his head. He leaned forward and kissed me gently.

"I could be asking you the same thing."

Thirty-Six

ALYSSA

For the better part of the next week, I lived out every girl's darkest, most forbidden fantasy. Because hopelessly snowed into a cozy cabin, in the mountains of Vermont... I was the sexual plaything for not one, but *three* ripped, gorgeous men.

The blizzard continued on and off for four days, raging just outside our snow-covered windows. By day two we couldn't even go outside. The drifts had covered the entire front door, so that when we opened it all we saw was a wall of pure white snow.

It was absolutely nuts. More snow than I'd ever seen in my life! In any other situation, it might even have been scary...

But not with the guys at my side.

We had enough food and water to keep us comfortable, and enough beer and wine if we rationed that too. Desmond and Mason carried in a metric shit-ton of firewood, while

Rogan and I stacked it neatly until it took up almost an entire wall.

The constantly-fed flames kept the cabin warm and toasty all day, even when the wind chill frosted everything outside. And at night...

Well, at night I had the guys to keep me warm.

They took me so often, and so deeply, my life became a steamy, sex-soaked wonderland. All throughout the house, I was fair game. My body was theirs to play with, whenever and wherever they wanted me.

And they wanted me often.

I lost count of the number of times I was dragged into a bedroom and screwed nearly senseless. Half the time I barely wore clothes! The cabin was so cozy I'd walk around barefoot, wearing a thong or G-string under a long T-shirt. We'd be playing a game or having a snack or just lounging around.. and then one of them would get this wild look in their eye. A look I grew to know very, *very* well.

A minute later I'd be bent over a couch or stood up and taken against a wall. Nailed hard from behind, or bounced onto someone's lap and impaled on one or more of their seemingly endless erections.

Because as much as I loved it, and was always ready? The guys were also in heat. There was a constant sexual tension hanging in the air at all times, and at any moment it boiled right over. One or more of us would just break off and start screwing like the whole world was coming to an end.

And judging from the weather outside, that might even be the case.

The Christmas Toy - Krista Wolf

I took Desmond and Rogan on the sofa, working them back and forth into a heated frenzy... only to be thrown down and screwed by Mason on the kitchen table. We screwed in every bedroom, every chair. I was nailed in the bathroom. Dragged into the coat closet. I was shoved face-down into a nest of blankets and pillows in front of the roaring fireplace, and tag-teamed spectacularly until tears of joy streaked down my cheeks.

I took a lot of hot showers, and I spent a lot of time on my knees. Every time someone wanted me, they had me in some form or another. I never said no. I never even came close.

For me, that was all part of the excitement, part of the game. Being available to them whenever they wanted me. Keeping all three of them wholly satisfied, whether together or alone. Fulfilling every single one of their fantasies, while at the same time, fulfilling mine.

In short, I loved becoming their *toy*.

And my God, the whole thing was just so incredibly hot. Being *used* by them, until the cabin constantly smelled of sex. Whatever we did, I was always dripping wet. We could be playing a board game, or sitting on the couch. Watching old movies on the cabin's ancient, stuttering VCR. It didn't matter, really. All that mattered was the delicious anticipation of being taken, which could come at any given time.

Not that I didn't do my fair share of initiating things as well. The sex toy inside me virtually every waking hour almost guaranteed I'd be ready. The smaller of the curved ends fit perfectly against my clit, holding it snugly in place while the egg-shaped part vibrated inside me.

The Christmas Toy - Krista Wolf

More than once, it made me jump them.

They took turns controlling it remotely, from their phones. Teasing me mercilessly, with a series of roller-coaster-like vibrations and thumping pulses that drove me absolutely crazy, at all different speeds.

I removed it when it got too much to bear, but the guys were always slipping it back in. It was a fun little game for them; seeing how fast they could make me come. Finding out which of them was better at using the app, and ultimately, using me, too.

I slept with Desmond, or between Mason and Rogan. And sometimes they slept with me. I'd wake up to find one or more of them pushing his way inside me, already stiff and hard. And I'd fuck them. I'd spread for one while staring into the eyes of his friend. I'd suck one while screwing down onto the other, while reaching out for the third like some crazed, sex-starved maniac.

The more I got, the more I needed it. The more *they* got, the more comfortable we all became. We would've gone stir crazy, if not for the sex. We peppered it in perfectly among the games and movies and general camaraderie of hanging together. Just me... and three of the sweetest, sexiest guys on the planet.

By the time the new year approached, I felt like the greediest bitch in the world.

Even worse, I could barely remember Florida at all. Our other lives seemed so distant, so far away. So totally unlike anything we had here, together, in our secluded little universe.

I knew one thing though, as I took them one, two,

even three at a time:

    Life would never be the same after this.

Thirty-Seven

MASON

Trapped in the cabin, unable to do anything for almost a week — it should've been simple, it should've been easy.

Instead, it was the craziest week of my life.

You'd think boiling life down to the basics would let you relax, especially after how busy the company had been this year. Eating. Drinking. Laughing. Fucking. These were the things that made up our lives. We started and ended our day the same way: usually between Alyssa's legs. Or with her between ours, waking us up in the best way possible. Smothering us beneath the sheets with her warm, curvy body...

Desmond's childhood movie collection turned out to be a treasure trove of amazing action movies, mainly from the 80's and 90's. We watched them on the living room's flat-panel television, marveling at how simple life used to be. How it seemed people had more of a connection with each other before technology *disconnected* them; phones, apps, the internet...

Of course, we had almost no phone service. During the storm, everything seemed to be on the fritz. We called our families for Christmas, but since then a tower must've gone down, leaving us in the dark. It was just as well, though. The more disconnected we became with the outside world, the more we seemed to concentrate on each other.

We learned that Alyssa had gone to Penn State. That she'd studied psychology, before switching her major. We learned that her family was just as disjointed as ours, her parents entirely disinterested in their children once they'd embraced their empty nest. To me, that seemed crazy. Having lost my mother at such a young age, and my father pretty much checking out? I couldn't wait to start a family of my own.

Desmond was the same way. He'd always been sort of a loner, which was the typical behavior for an only child. Yet he'd had a strong sense of family, even when he didn't have one. He treated Rogan and I like the brothers he never had, and we welcomed him with open arms.

That's why it didn't seem strange at all when we'd embraced Alyssa. Unorthodox maybe, but the whole relationship that blossomed between us had the elements of a family dynamic to it. There was respect. Camaraderie. Rivalry. Even love. And yeah, that last part seemed a little crazy the first time it passed through my head. But at the same time, did it *really?*

You care about her.

That was natural. An emotional closeness was almost inevitable, especially considering how physically close we'd become.

No, you care about her a LOT.

It was a nagging thought, racing through the back of my mind. Maybe not so nagging, though. Nagging held an intrusively negative connotation, and my feelings for Alyssa were anything but that.

It was more like a welcome thought, actually.

I thought of these things as I sat sipping my beer, gazing up at our beautiful Christmas tree. It looked majestic — especially at night — and so much better than the flimsy piece of plastic from the attic we usually put up. It made the whole cabin smell like pine, too. Which in turn, smelled like Christmas.

We'd been coming here for years, the three of us. At first alone, and then with Emma too. It was always fun. Always a good time, both before and after Desmond had started sharing Emma's affections with us, on every possible level.

But this year...

There was something about this year that just felt different. Everything was more vibrant, more alive. And we'd done less this year than in previous years for sure. We'd only been up on the mountain twice. And aside from hitting the town a few times, we hadn't done any of the side activities we'd talked about doing. Not even the snowmobiling we enjoyed so much each year.

The blizzard had limited our options for sure. But even beyond that, we just wanted to *be* here. Alyssa had brought nothing but good vibes with her. Her happiness and optimism were infectious, her enthusiasm as adorable as she was.

Sexual exploits aside, she made us want to be around her in all new ways. And although I'd never admit it to Desmond, they were ways that Emma never had.

There were a lot of things I couldn't put my finger on, but that part was easy. Alyssa was a *lot* more laid back. She took to our situation like a fish to water, and she rolled with whatever punches came her way. I knew this about her from working alongside her, but it was even more apparent here, sharing all this time with her. In short, she was just... cooler. As well as tons more flexible.

That part, Rogan and I had already discussed. Without Desmond of course, because, well...

Boom!

It was just after lunch and we were lounging around, when the master bedroom door abruptly slammed open. We all looked up at once as Alyssa came storming down the hall. Her face was flush, her eyes alive with sudden excitement.

"What is it?" Desmond asked in alarm. "What's wrong?"

Alyssa was holding a book — Emma's journal. It dangled from the end of one slender arm as her face broke into a disbelieving grin.

"There's a *hot tub* in the back yard?"

Thirty-Eight

ALYSSA

I couldn't believe it! Or rather, I hoped beyond all hope it was still true. That they hadn't removed it. That it hadn't broken down, or—

"No," Desmond answered mechanically, dashing my hopes. "I mean, not that we can get to. Not now, of course."

"But it's still back there?"

He shrugged a shoulder. "Technically, yes."

My spirits wanted to soar, but my mind was holding them back. Still hesitant.

"And it *works?*"

"Well... if we fired it up, yeah. Sort of. I mean—"

"What he means is it's buried under six feet of snow," said Rogan.

"Way back there, too," Mason added. "All the way in the far corner of the yard."

The three of them sounded defeatist. I hated defeatist.

"Well then let's dig it out."

Desmond's mouth dropped open. Rogan laughed.

"Honey, it's way, *way* back there," said Mason, placatingly. "Too far to reach. Plus, we'd have to uncover the mechanicals. It'll need water. The hose is frozen..."

"We could thaw out the hose inside," Rogan countered. "That part's easy."

I felt a glimmer of hope dawn. I looked eagerly at Desmond.

"We have shovels, don't we?"

"Two of them," said Mason. "Yeah."

"So we take turns," I said. "We dig our way out to it. Uncover it. Fill it up..."

"We'd have to dig out the wood-fired heater too," said Desmond. "Get that running." He sighed and shook his head. "But it would take so much time just to—"

"Time is something we have lots of," I pointed out. "What the hell else are we doing?"

The guys looked at each other briefly. Slowly, all of them grinned.

"Besides *that*."

"Nothing I guess," Desmond shrugged.

"It would be nice to get away from the cabin for a bit," Mason admitted. "Even if it's just twenty yards away."

"Hey," said Rogan. "It's outside. Fresh air. New

surroundings."

"Plus it's a hot tub," I jumped in. "Can you imagine how good that'll feel?"

My heart was racing now. The anticipation of actually doing something outside — much less hanging out beneath the stars — was sending a welcome surge of adrenaline through my body.

"It's an apocalyptic wasteland out there," said Rogan, scratching his head. He turned to Desmond. "If we tunneled out, you think we could hit it?"

Desmond was looking at me, perhaps feeding off my excitement. I thought I detected the slightest hint of a smile.

"Yeah," he said. "I know where it is."

"So we'll try?" I asked excitedly.

They rose, and I knew I had them. One by one they began stretching, while staring me down.

"Think of all the things you can *do* to me in that hot tub," I purred. "Wet things. Delicious things..."

Mason grabbed the shovels and placed them near the back door. He and Rogan peeled off to get dressed, leaving Desmond and I face to face.

"Bundle up," he told me, nodding toward the hallway. "I can't promise anything, but we can give it a shot."

Thirty-Nine

ALYSSA

"Alright!" Rogan cried, nodding to us from atop a mound of snow. "Fire it up!"

Desmond hit the ignitor, and I saw the spark. Flames engulfed the stack of wood and kindling inside the shiny steel drum. Through the tiny observation pane I could see it begin glowing yellow, and then orange.

"Shit," breathed Mason, through a puff of frozen white smoke. "It worked."

"Damn straight!" Rogan declared gleefully. He jumped down from one side of what had become our snow-trench, his stubbled cheeks bright red from the cold. "First try, too."

We'd opened the back door to a smooth wall of whiteness — so much that it actually made us laugh. Then we began chopping away. We worked in pairs, digging into the seemingly endless pile of snow. Creating a tunnel that was dark at first, but grew brighter with moonlight as we broke through the ceiling and exposed our trench to the sky.

It had taken us *hours.* How many, I didn't know. The sun had set long ago by the time we reached the slatted wall of the hot tub. We dug along the sides in a square, creating a path all around it, before climbing on top and digging out the cover.

The whole time, I couldn't help but watch the guys. The way they moved, the way they worked as one. How hot it was, seeing them set to the task of manual labor. Watching their muscles strain against their winter clothing, until they were so hot they were peeling parts of it off.

And then after that, watching them actually *sweat.*

I'd seen them naked and aroused, their hard muscles flexing and rolling beneath their skin as they'd gone to work on my eager body. Still, it was just as hot seeing *this.* At the office they all sat behind desks. I'd flirted with guys in button-down shirts who worked financial spreadsheets and drew architectural plans and made phone calls to clients.

But this... this was heaven.

"What now?" I asked eagerly. We were so close to our goal, I didn't want to jinx anything.

"Now we wait," Mason replied, "for the water to get up to temperature."

"Which would be—"

"Three or four hours," said Desmond. "Give or take."

I tried not to look disappointed. "Oh."

"Hey," Desmond said, touching my chin. "It *should* take eight or twelve. Lucky for us, the old heater went a couple years back. I replaced it with this newer, kickass model."

"Okay," I smiled. "Sorry, if I sound impatient."

"Don't be," he said, smiling back. "It's cute."

He held my hands and kissed me in the sanctity of our trench, surrounded by snow on both sides. Like the rest of us, his body was freezing. But his lips were warm and welcoming.

"Besides, it gives us time for dinner."

Dinner! I didn't even have the slightest clue what time it was. All I knew was that the moon was out, making everything glimmer and shimmer. My body was sweaty and spent and exhausted, but yet I was exhilarated at the same time.

"Leftovers probably," Desmond shrugged. "But I'll bet we're more hungry than we realize."

My hand slipped from his as he headed back to the house. Just then, Rogan swept past me. He took me into his arms and kissed me as well; an even deeper, more meaningful kiss that had me instantly light on my feet.

Wow...

There was something about kissing outside, with the icy air biting at every inch of my exposed skin, that made the whole thing more intimate. I snuggled into him. Kissed him right back with equal fervor, my tongue questing for his as my hand reached up to scratch at his reassuringly stubbly face.

"Thanks for backing me up," I murmured, sighing into his mouth.

"On what?"

"On the whole hot tub thing."

Rogan only grinned and kissed me some more. "Hey, I wanted it as bad as you did."

My eyes went wide. "You *did?*"

"Hell yeah," he chuckled.

"Then why didn't you—"

"Because Desmond wouldn't have done it for me. For you however..." he winked, "it's an entirely different story."

We kissed some more, until suddenly—

"Hey, save some for me!"

Mason was next, practically lifting me from Rogan's grasp and taking instant possession of me. His grasp was strong and wonderful as he lifted me into his arms.

"She belongs to all of us, remember?"

He slipped his gloves off, then took my cold face in his warm hands. It felt so good I sighed out loud, as he closed his mouth hotly over mine.

She belongs to us...

The words were territorial. Dominating, but without jealousy.

And shit, they turned me on.

I'm really theirs.

It occurred to me for the first time that maybe we'd crossed a threshold. Gone past the point of me being their Christmas toy, and ventured into all new territory of... well...

Of what, actually?

I really didn't know. All I knew was the sensation of being protected and cared for, even loved. That explosion of butterflies, whenever they held me. That whatever feelings of ownership or possessiveness or guardianship over me that the guys felt...

The feeling was entirely mutual.

"YO!"

Rogan's voice carried down the trench, muted against the big snow walls. We were still making out like lost lovers when it reached our ears. Still kissing.

"When you guys are finished, come in and eat!"

Forty

ALYSSA

"Holy shit holy shit holy SHIT!"

I was running full speed. Sprinting straight down our icy snow tunnel, which Rogan had started referring to as the Hoth-trench. If my legs were cold, my feet were absolutely freezing! For some stupid reason, I'd left my boots in the cabin.

"Hurry up! Just get in!"

I climbed the makeshift steps, then shrugged out of my robe. The frozen air hit my naked body full blast, covering me with goosebumps, stippling my skin in a nanosecond.

"No no, hang on," said Rogan, putting his hand up.

"What? What?"

"She should take her time," he smiled, ogling my shivering body. "No reason to rush into—"

"The hell with that!"

Guided by Desmond's and Rogan's hands, I stepped

forward and lowered myself into the bubbling hot tub. The swirling, steaming water wasn't just incredible, it was absolutely life-changing.

"OHHHHHHHHHHH..."

It was the best orgasm in the world, knitted into a blanket, wrapped around every inch of my body.

"Holy SHIT..."

I sank in up to my neck, wincing in absolute euphoria. The cold had vanished in an instant. Everything was just immediately and irrevocably comfortable.

"Beer?"

I opened my eyes. Desmond was handing me one of the ice cold beers, plucked out of the snow. The cap was already off. I took it and drank deeply, feeling the satisfying rush of cool liquid splash in the pit of my heated stomach.

"To hell with blizzards," I said, kicking back into my spot. "Maybe we should just stay here forever."

The others chuckled knowingly. Each of them had their own little corner of the hot tub.

"Forever huh?" asked Rogan.

"Oh yeah."

"We'd run out of food eventually," said Mason.

"Bah. Food's overrated."

Desmond raised an eyebrow. "Water?"

I waved him away. "We can drink the melted snow."

For the next half minute the guys said nothing, as a

blissful silence settled over our surroundings. Above us, the night-blue sky was about as clear as could be. Except for the moon... and about a billion twinkling stars.

"I guess I'd eventually run out of birth control," I sighed finally.

Desmond laughed. "*That* could pose a problem."

"A serious problem, yeah."

The water was beyond relaxing. It soothed our tired muscles. Even though it was already past midnight, it made all the time and effort worthwhile.

"Here's to you," said Rogan raising his bottle my way.

"Me?"

"If it weren't for you, we never would've dug our way out here."

I clinked his bottle against mine. "Here's to that journal in my nighttable," I countered. "If not for all the things I read about in there... I wouldn't even know there *was* a hot tub."

The guys looked at each other, probably wondering what part of their past lives I'd read about. Which of the many nights they'd spent in the hot tub that Emma felt the need to document.

"You spend a lot of time reading that journal," said Desmond abruptly.

"Yeah. So?"

He took a long pull from his beer, and stared straight ahead. "So maybe don't worry so much about the past?"

My eyebrows knitted together. "What?"

"I mean, rather than follow in Emma's footsteps," he said placidly, "maybe worry more about walking your own path?"

The thought hadn't occurred to me: exactly how Desmond felt about me reading his ex-girlfriend's journal. I just assumed that it was okay, especially since it led to us all being together. But now...

Now I realized there was something else there. Regret, maybe. Or even a lost opportunity.

"I think it's high time you told me something," I said, being sure to look at each of them in turn. "Something important."

Their attention was focused on me now. Wondering what came next.

"I know what you did with her," I continued. "When it started, and how long it went on. But I need the details. I need more info."

They stared back at me through the steam, their eyes reflecting the starlight.

"Tell me what happened with Emma..."

Forty-One

DESMOND

She gazed back at us from her corner of the tub, looking relaxed but in command. Even with her hair matted against her face, she was utterly beautiful. In fact, it kinda made the whole thing even sexier.

"What do you want to know?"

"You can tell me how it started, first," she said, looking directly at me. "How the two of you got into this as a couple. What was said between you. What was discussed. And how two turned into four..."

She wasn't prying here, she was genuinely interested. And considering our circumstances, if anyone had a right to know... it was her.

"Well it was a fantasy at first," I said.

"Yours or hers?"

"Both, really," I shrugged. "I mean Emma was always pretty open-minded. When you watch enough porn together, the one-on-one scenes become boring. You start venturing out. Checking into the 2-on-1 stuff."

I could see her nodding, understanding. Commiserating even, as if she'd encountered the same scenario with an ex-boyfriend or two.

"We started the whole 'would you do this... would you do that...' conversation. Always in bed, of course. Mainly while we were making love, and we were both worked up."

My eyes narrowed as I tried to gauge Alyssa's reaction. She looked like she was getting redder, possibly from the steam.

"You sure you wanna hear all this?"

"Yes," she said immediately. "Definitely."

"Well, we started bringing up the idea of a third person. One of her girlfriends maybe, although she didn't know who. And there was a jealousy there, whenever we mentioned it. Even as a fantasy, I could tell she would have somewhat of a problem sharing me with another girl."

She finished her beer, then turned to Rogan and asked for another. He pulled one from where it sat neck-deep in the snow and handed it over.

"Go on."

"After that, most of the movies we chose started involving two guys and one girl," I said. "Not that I minded, really. I started getting into the idea. The whole sharing aspect. How hot it would be to watch her with someone else. Sucking them off. Getting taken..."

I felt my own flush of excitement, remembering those times. How hot Emma had gotten, whenever we talked about it.

"I'd make up scenarios while we were screwing and say them out loud," I said. "Or whisper into her ear all the things we could do if there were another guy there. It made us both hot. Hot enough that we started exploring... options."

"And you weren't jealous at the idea of sharing her?" Alyssa asked. "Like she was?"

She was bright red now, and I knew it wasn't just from the hot tub. Alyssa was getting worked up. She was getting off on hearing all this.

"Actually the more I thought about it the hotter it was for me," I admitted. "And since there was zero jealousy on my end, I agreed to try it."

"So you picked your friends," she asked.

"Yes. Rather than strangers."

"I see."

"Or rather, Emma picked them," I admitted. "She'd always been attracted to Rogan. She was always flirting with Mason. I made up scenarios involving one and then the other, and she got off equally to both of them." I shrugged again. "At that point I realized it didn't matter. That either one could fulfill the fantasy for us, and all we had to do was ask."

Rogan screwed the cap off another pair of beers. He handed me one and smiled.

"That's where I came in," he said proudly. "One night at the bar after we'd had way too many, this asshole asks me if I think his girlfriend is hot." He grinned sheepishly. "Of course I said yes. Emma was cute as hell, but it was still a little weird to be answering that question from your best friend."

I laughed, looking across at my friend. "And then things got a lot weirder. Because I asked him if he'd like to fuck her."

"No," Rogan corrected him. "You asked me if I'd like to *help* you fuck her. That's how you worded it."

"Shit, that's right," I laughed. "Man, you remember *everything*, don't you?"

"Yeah, well when your best friend asks you to bang his old lady, it's not something you usually forget."

Alyssa let out a short laugh, and I took it as a good sign. She was still entranced, though. And I noticed the hand not holding her beer had surreptitiously disappeared beneath the swirling, churning water.

"After that it was just a matter of where and when," I said. "We tried to hook up around Thanksgiving at my apartment, but the three of us got too drunk. We pushed it off another week or three, and then suddenly it was time to go to the cabin. And when Emma suggested she tag along, 'to get this thing done', it seemed only natural that we invite her."

"Natural to you guys," Mason jumped in. "By this point, I didn't know jack shit about it."

Rogan laughed. "Not yet anyway," he said. "But we eventually dragged you into the whole sordid affair."

Mason smirked and tipped his bottle. "No dragging required, really."

"And how did *that* happen?" asked Alyssa. Her voice was low and tight. A little breathless.

"Desmond and I got him drunk the night before we left," Rogan admitted. "When we figured he'd had enough beers, we told him everything. And... well..."

"At that point we knew he had to be involved," I said. "And I figured the best way to break that to Emma, would be to have him 'walk in' on us, in the middle of the act."

"And then join in," said Alyssa. "Just like in the journal."

"Exactly."

Rogan took a quick swig and shook his head, grinning. "She *knew*, bro. I don't care what you say."

Mason nodded in agreement. "By the look in her eyes, I'd have to say yeah. I was standing in that doorway all of a few seconds before she invited me over. And it wasn't like you guys could do something like that and keep it from me. Not in *this* place, and certainly not for a week and a half."

We were all staring at Alyssa now, and she was staring right back. For a few long seconds, everything went silent.

"So it wasn't a one-time thing," she stated flatly.

"I guess originally it was supposed to be," I shrugged. "We really hadn't gotten that far. Only she enjoyed it so much she wanted to do it again. And again after that."

"I'd say you *both* enjoyed it," Rogan corrected me.

I laughed. "And you guys didn't?"

"Fine," he conceded. "We all had a pretty fun time. And we were all stuck with each other through the holiday, so we spent it... well... you know."

"Oh I know," said Alyssa. "I read *all* about it. I know

it went on even after you got back to Florida. And it kept happening year after year, until you broke up."

She looked back at me carefully, taking her time. I knew the next question before she asked it.

"So why'd she—"

"Break up with me?"

She nodded slowly, drawing her bottle back to her lips.

"Emma got flighty," I said. "She wanted to move out west — Vegas maybe, or California. She told me to come with her. No, scratch that. She *demanded* that I come with her."

"Why didn't you?"

"Because I'm doing well for myself here, in her father's company," I said. "I used to run crews. It took years for me to work my way into the air-conditioned office, and now I run several projects at once, from the comfort of a nice desk."

I shrugged, remembering. "I wasn't about to throw it all away. Emma couldn't understand that, though. Her father had taken care of her her whole life — including the cushy office job where she did virtually nothing. She didn't know the value of money, or the struggle of paying bills, or what it was like to be short on the rent. She was immature that way. Selfish."

"More like self-centered," said Rogan. "But yeah. Blind to the wills of the world."

"So she just... left you?" asked Alyssa. "She left *all* of you?"

"Well she left me, that's for sure," I chuckled. "As for these clowns... well, for Emma it was always just sex."

"Us too," laughed Rogan, and Mason nodded. "Sorry man."

"Don't be," I told him. "I knew what it was from the moment it happened. And even though it went on for a long time, it was just never anything different."

Alyssa was searching my expression now. Trying to determine if I were being genuine, or if she were only hearing the bitter words of a jilted lover.

It didn't take long for her to figure which it really was.

"Same thing with me I guess," she said softly. "I might not be anyone's girlfriend, but it's just a bunch of se—"

"NO."

It was a single word, but it stopped her immediately from finishing her sentence. And that was probably because the word had come from all three of our mouths at the same time.

"It's not the same thing with you at *all*," Rogan said.

Mason nodded. "Not even close."

I reached out across the swirling water, and she took my hand. It was an easy thing to pull her in. To feel the silky smoothness of her naked legs sliding around either side of me, as I settled her snugly into my lap.

"With you it's different," I told her. "Way different."

Her body was pressed tightly against mine. I could feel her heart pounding away! Hammering wildly within her chest.

"With Emma, everything was all about her," I went on. "Always was. Always will be." I shook my head slowly. "But not you. Never you."

I took her face in my hands. I made her look upward, past the dripping curtain of hair that flopped over her forehead, and straight into my eyes.

"You belong to *all* of us," I said softly. "We all started together. We started equal."

Rogan was on her left now. Mason on her right. Their hands went to her body, moving with deliberate affection. Stroking her cheek gently. Pulling her hair from her face.

"It's not just sex anymore," I whispered. "Not for me."

I kissed her tenderly, and I could swear I felt her heart skip a beat.

"Not for any of us."

Forty-Two

ALYSSA

He felt absolutely enormous inside me. Bigger and more swollen than ever before, as I bounced happily on Desmond's lap.

"That's it baby..."

I was riding him up and down beneath the superheated water. Grinding into his groin, with my arms locked tightly over his big, granite shoulders.

But the whole time, I took turns kissing his two friends.

This is...

Six hands roamed my body. Three hungry mouths, kissing me all over as I writhed and twisted between my three gorgeous lovers.

...the best night of my life.

I'd never thought anything could feel this good before. The sense of being outside, with the cold winter air biting at my exposed skin. Surrounded by snow... sky... the wilderness; giant fragrant pines, looming at the edge of darkness.

And yet not being the least bit cold, because I was wholly *enveloped* in hot flesh.

I was kissing Mason. Stroking Rogan. Taking Desmond all the way inside my body, his firm hands squeezing my hips beneath the hot tub's roiling, bubbling surface.

"Give her here."

I was passed to the next lover — Mason this time — settling down into his lap with my back to him. I felt his hand, guiding himself inside me. Sliding that monster way up inside me, aided by my own silky wetness, deep in my heated channel.

"*Fuuuuck,*" he swore, drawing the word out. "I'll never get tired of that."

Desmond was kissing me now, holding my face in his hands. My breasts were above the water, everything all stiff from the cold. The contrast was amazing, especially when Rogan took one into his hot mouth. I sighed as he closed his warm palm over the other one.

"You just gonna go back and forth?" Desmond whispered nastily into my ear. "Like a little slut?"

He'd been saying all kinds of stuff like this, since the moment we started. It was so hot it brought things to all new levels.

"I *am* a slut..." I whispered back, playing the game. "Aren't I?"

"You're *our* slut, yes."

"Mmmm..." I purred, smiling. "I *love* that you said that."

He kissed me again, just as I sighed and rolled my hips. It felt so good I wanted to scream.

My God!

This was way beyond sex, now. It was more like a religious experience. I'd never felt more safe, more happy, more secure. More well-taken care of, and attended to, and surrounded by warmth and love and—

Mason surged upward, and grunted into my other ear. I knew the grunt well. He was about to lose it.

"I want you to explode..." I moaned, tilting my chin his way. "Can you do that for me? My pussy's ready."

It had been ready for a long time now. I'd come three times, once on each of them. They'd made sure it went down that way, switching me off after it happened. Trading me in a circle, like some dirty little possession, until I'd screwed down and erupted with all three of them inside me.

"*Fill* me," I growled, planting a kiss on Mason's cheek. His head was over my shoulder now. I could see the intensity in his expression, as he struggled to keep from sailing over the edge. "Don't hold back, honey. Just let it go..."

He grunted and shoved forward, driving himself all the way home. It sent me upward in his lap, my hands resting on the coiled muscles of his powerful thighs.

Holy shit...

Desmond had stood up in front of me, his magnificent body glistening in the moonlight. He held himself in one big fist. Guiding himself down my throat.

"Suck it, baby."

I did it eagerly, hungrily. Grasping it with one hand, balancing with the other. He leaned forward a little, driving himself deeper as he placed his lips against my ear.

"Suck me off while my best friend *comes* in you..."

That was it — and I didn't even know it. Another orgasm ripped through me, surging up from completely out of nowhere. It happened just as Mason exploded, my sheath milking him in spasm after glorious spasm as he throbbed and pulsed and filled me with his cream.

It didn't make sense, how something like this could happen. Two weeks ago I was looking forward to absolutely nothing. Ready to hit a few relatively tame Christmas parties, while enjoying a boring week off from work.

And now...

FUCKKKKK...

It was pleasure mixed with pain. Waves of searing hot ecstasy, edged with the feeling of being stretched past the point of comfortability. But I had no time to focus on that place deep in my belly, where Mason and I were joined beneath the water. And that's because Desmond's hands sifted into my hair, his shaft twitching crazily as he exploded down my throat.

"*Unghhh!*"

His grunt was primal, almost pre-historic. My eyes fluttered open, and I could see every ripple of his washboard stomach come alive.

God, that's so damned ho—

My cheeks bowed out as Desmond kept coming and coming, filling my mouth. I couldn't understand where it was originating from. I'd kept all three of my boys well-taken care of.

At the last second he threw his head to the midnight sky. I thought he was going to howl like a wolf, but instead he only roared:

"God, I LOVE this!"

I almost laughed, but at the moment I was a little preoccupied. It was cute. Funny. Hilarious even, especially when the other two laughed.

Eventually I slid from Mason's lap, wondering if I'd been broken. But with Rogan sliding himself right back inside me, I didn't have to wonder long.

"I'm gonna need some of whatever that was," he chuckled.

The others slid back to their corners, finally sated, stretching their great arms along the length of the hot tub. I heard them sigh contentedly as they watched their friend rhythmically screw my hot, come-filled entrance.

Delirious with happiness, riding up and down in Rogan's lap, I looked over his shoulder at them and laughed.

Mason and Desmond's eyes narrowed.

"What?"

"And to think," I smiled back at them, "I was worried about being a fifth wheel..."

Forty-Three

ALYSSA

Desmond plowed the driveway two mornings later. New Year's Eve dawned bright and blue and totally brilliant, and the guys shoveled their way to the truck before I was finished making us all breakfast with the last of our food.

It was a good thing, not only because we were running out of supplies — we were also going stir-crazy. All four of us had a serious case of cabin fever. The hot tub had been a godsend, giving us a chance to get outside a little bit for the past two days. But we needed more. We needed to get off the property and see other places, other people.

Two more days...

That's all we had together. Our flight was scheduled for Thursday morning, and by that evening we'd be back in our respective apartments in Florida. Back to reality.

God, it's going to be so weird.

I laughed a little, but the laughter came with a lump in my throat. It was surprising how fast such a crazy situation could become the norm. And how everyday life could seem so foreign, compared to the last week and a half.

On one hand I was looking forward to being home. To seeing how our relationship might develop once we were back at the office, and back to our normal routines.

On the other hand, I was terrified.

The four of us had spent every waking moment together for a long time now. But since that initial night in the hot tub, things had grown even more intense.

And intense wasn't even a strong enough word.

The guys had taken to showing me more affection than ever, on individual levels as well as together. I'd spent time with each of them. One by one, they'd crawled beneath my covers. First Mason, then Desmond, then Rogan; they'd slept in my bed, curled up against me. Cuddling me for hours at a clip, just one-on-one.

And we'd made *love*, too. That was really the only word for it. One at a time they'd climbed over me, or pulled me onto their hard, muscle-bound bodies. They screwed me slowly, each of them kissing me deeply, hotly, until we were totally delirious with want and desire. Staring into my eyes as our passion built to an emotional crescendo, before climaxing together as they spent themselves between my legs.

I woke up to walk the cabin at night, marveling at how perfect everything had been. Standing naked in front of the fire. Letting the heat wash over me, soaking it in down to my bones. I'd gone over every moment with each of them in my mind, while staring out the snow-kissed window and wondering what came next. At one point a pair of arms had slid around me — Rogan, kissing my shoulder. Calling me back to bed, with his warm body pressed up against my back.

I loved it here. Everything about the place. But of course, it was all about the guys...

"You ready?"

Desmond held the door for me as I hopped into the truck. As it rumbled down the freshly-plowed driveway and broke into the street, all four of us cheered.

"We're free!" cried Rogan.

"Hell yeah," Mason laughed.

We headed straight into town, which looked absolutely breathtaking all covered in snow. Only half the shops had been dug out. And only half of those were actually open.

"Food. Drink." Desmond made his own makeshift parking spot, right beside a great mound of snow. "Those are our priorities."

We spent the afternoon buying whatever we needed to restock the cabin, but not too much in the way of perishables. After all, we were leaving in a couple of days. Desmond had words with a few of the locals, while the rest of us hung back. They caught him up on a lot of things, and he returned looking a little more serious than when he left.

"We've got a little bit of a change of plan..."

We listened as he went to explain how much of the town was still in some dire straits. There were people stranded. Some without food.

"It would be a big help if I plowed things out for the rest of the day," he said. He nodded toward his friends. "And if you guys took up some shovels."

The men on either side of me both shrugged. "We could do that," Rogan said.

"Good," Desmond grinned. "Because I already told them you would."

"You've got a shovel for me I hope," I butted in. But Desmond shook his head.

"I need you back home," he said. "Keep the fire going. Maybe shovel some of the snow away from the side of the cabin, so the pipes don't freeze."

I stared back at them a little wounded, but realized he was right. If anyone was hanging back, it would need to be me. I knew firsthand the three of them could move some *serious* snow.

Besides it felt strangely good, Desmond calling it 'home'.

"You still get to shovel," Rogan offered with a hopeful grin.

"Alright."

"Thanks baby," said Desmond with a smile. "Hop in, I'll drop you off."

Rogan and Mason hugged me before leaving, probably because if they both kissed me in front of the locals they'd faint straight away. That was one of the things I hadn't considered about potentially having three boyfriends. The optics of everything.

"We still on for tonight?" I asked, a bit hesitantly.

We'd planned to go to the Spruce Creek lodge for the New Year's Eve celebration, at the base of the mountain. Ring in 2020 with a few drinks and some champagne. And of course, kisses at midnight.

"Oh yeah," said Desmond. "No matter what."

"Because I understand if you aren't," I said sympathetically. "You know, if you guys get tired from all the shoveling and plowing—"

"We're staying till' midnight at the very least," interrupted Rogan. "Don't worry."

"Okay," I said happily. "We don't have to stay very long afterward. In fact, maybe I could, you know..." I paused demurely. "*Incentivize* you boys to leave."

The guys huddled around me in silence for a moment, exchanging glances.

"We're listening," said Rogan.

"A round of ice cold beers and fireside blowjobs?" I chuckled.

Mason grinned. Desmond whistled.

"Dunno about you guys, but I'm sold."

We laughed together and I climbed into the truck, already looking forward to our little after-party.

You're bad, Alyssa... very bad!

I watched the locals hand Rogan and Mason a pair of shovels as we pulled away. It was a heartwarming sight. It felt good that we could be of some help.

Desmond drove me back uneventfully, plowing our driveway once more as he dropped me at the cabin's front door. Our goodbye kiss in the front of the cab turned into an impromptu, two-minute makeout session. If we'd let it go on any longer, I would've dragged him into the house and jumped him.

"Be back a little later," he said. "Keep that fire roaring. Stay inside after it gets dark, and don't forget to lock the door."

"Yes dad," I giggled.

I waved him down the driveway before pushing into the cabin. The second the door shut behind me, the entire place was blanketed by silence.

"Ah," I said into the emptiness. "Home sweet home."

The atmosphere was a little strange, really. It occurred to me this was the first time I'd been all alone since the trip began.

You live *alone,* I reminded myself. *Remember?*

I set immediately to task, putting away the things we'd bought and then feeding the fire. I'd learned a lot from watching Mason. I knew how to layer the logs, and how to poke down the embers to allow more oxygen. I even ventured out back and brought in a few more choice pieces of wood, as the wall we'd stacked a week ago was running seriously low.

I was warming my hands and feeling particularly proud of myself when I heard a sharp knock at the door.

There wasn't a peephole. Hell, I didn't even think twice. The people up here had all been so nice, so neighborly, I didn't even consider who or what could be on the side.

I just opened it...

To find a young woman standing there, holding a bag. Somewhere behind her, a car was just pulling away.

"Er... hi," she said, considering me very strangely. Her brows knit together... just as a light of recognition flipped on in my mind.

"Is Desmond here?"

Forty-Four

ALYSSA

The woman before me was smaller and waifish, with dark hair and shrewd, almond-shaped eyes. She poked her head past me to look inside the cabin, and my hand clapped involuntarily over my mouth.

Emma.

Oh my God, I was staring at Emma! The boss's daughter. The girl who'd worked in the office with us for a time, but who I really hadn't paid much attention to.

"Hey..."

The one who'd dated Desmond... and maybe technically even Rogan, and Mason, too.

"Where *is* everyone?"

The one who wrote the *journal.*

Holy SHIT!

"Hello!" Emma said, snapping her fingers in the general direction of my face. "Did you hear me? I asked you a question."

God, she was here not even ten seconds and I already wanted to punch her.

"W—What?"

"Where. Is. Desmond?" she repeated, all annoyed. "And Rogan, and Mason—"

"They're in town," I said quickly. "Shoveling."

She looked at me like she didn't believe me. "*Shoveling?*"

"And plowing, yeah. They kinda got caught up in—"

Emma pushed straight past me, dragging her oversized carry-on into the cabin. She glanced around, her eyes darting everywhere at once. Her gaze fell on the fire, on the decorations... then on the tree.

"What the—"

She stormed over, looking our tree up and down. Cradling one of the ornaments in her palm. Kicking beneath it, at the root ball. She even snapped one of the branches off, between her fingers.

Now I *really* wanted to kick her ass.

"Do you know when they'll be back?" she asked, with mock sweetness.

"N—No," I stammered. "Not really."

"Desmond's not answering his phone," she said, walking the cabin in a tight circle. "None of them are."

She peered out through the back window, and noticed the path we'd dug to the hot tub. My heart was pounding! I had no idea what to do.

"You can go now," she said suddenly, without even looking back at me.

Her body language was different now. It had gone from annoyance to remembrance to... well... something else entirely.

"I can *what?*"

"You came here to clean the cabin, right?" she said plainly, making more of a factual statement than asking a question. "And I'm telling you don't worry about it. You can take off now."

"But—"

"Don't worry sweetie," she added. "I'll tell Desmond you did your job."

"I'm *not* the cleaning lady," I said, clearing my throat.

Emma turned to regard me again, this time in an all new light. She looked me over head to toe.

"Then what are you—"

"I came up here with the guys. On the trip."

I watched as her eyes grew wider and wider, until I thought they were going to pop out of her skull. Shit, it was actually enjoyable.

"You *what?*"

"I came skiing," I shrugged, then folded my arms. "They invited me. We all had Christmas together."

Emma's head turned, like it was on a swivel. "Who are you with? Rogan or Mason?"

"Neither."

Anger flared, somewhere behind her eyes. "You're with *Desmond?*"

"No," I said, probably a little too quickly. "I'm from the office. I *worked* with you, Emma. Well, maybe not with you but at least alongside you."

For some reason she seemed astounded by the news. She was looking back at me like I had sixteen heads.

"You're the boss's daughter, Emma. I know who you are."

For a few seconds she just stood there, totally at a loss. Then she pushed past me for a second time. I looked on in fear as she stomped her way down the hall.

Oh shit!

The journal had been on the nightstand all week. There'd been no reason to hide it anymore. No reason to put it away...

"Emma, wait!"

I reached for her. I almost even grabbed her arm. But she was too fast, too quick. She ran down the hall like she was trying to catch me in something. I didn't know what, until—

"WHAT THE FUCK!?"

I rushed into the master bedroom, my heart stuck in my throat. Emma was just inside the doorway, staring at my suitcase.

"So you *are* with Desmond!" she whirled on me. "You're staying in our *room!*"

Relief flooded through me. She hadn't seen the journal yet.

"They gave *me* the master," I countered. "I'm staying here alone." I edged past her, positioning myself between the nighttable and her line of vision. "Desmond's staying in that room," I pointed. "Mason and Rogan are—"

She ran out without another word, to check the side bedrooms. Overwhelmed with relief, I shoved at the book blindly with one hand. I felt it slide off the nighttable, wedging itself between the table and the wall.

Thank. God.

Emma checked both rooms, where she found the guys' clothing and personal items. I saw her shoulders relax a little, but not much.

"I told you we're just friends," I explained quickly. "Co-workers. The four of us came up here to ski and hang out."

She stared daggers back at me. I realized right then there was no convincing her.

"Emma, do the guys know you're *here?*"

Her lips curled back in a sneer. If her mouth could've dripped venom, she would've.

"The *guys?*"

I shrugged, not understanding. "Yeah. I mean—"

"Who the hell are *you* to call them 'the guys'?" she snarled.

She paused, and suddenly our eyes locked. I could see her trying to read me. Looking past what my lips were saying...

and diving straight into my head.

Uh oh.

The wheels were turning, but I dared not look down. Instead I held her gaze. The two of us locked in the worst of all possible staring contests, until—

"You're not with one of them..." she said suddenly, her voice breaking.

I bit my tongue and swallowed hard. Emma's eyes narrowed, glassing over with tears.

"You're with *all* of them."

Up until now I'd been defensive. Maybe I'd even felt a bit sorry for her. But now? Now I was getting pissed.

"Excuse me?"

"You came here on *my* plane ticket," she spat acidly, "with *my* boyfriend and his friends. Then you have the balls to stay in our room. To sleep in *our* bed..."

"He's *not* your boyfriend."

Emma's face twisted in a grimace of pain. I could've stabbed her in the chest and she would've given me less of a dirty look.

"You broke up with him, remember?" I went on. "Plus this is *his* cabin. *His* bed. If he was nice enough to lend me the master, and the others were kind enough to have me along on their trip, I don't see what business it is of—"

BOOM!

A rush of air blew my hair back as the door before me slammed violently shut. It was followed by the click of the latch engaging, as Emma locked herself securely in Desmond's room.

Forty-Five

ALYSSA

"Alright... where is she?"

I pointed to his doorway, as Desmond stepped past me. The others walked in behind him, all covered in ice and blown snow.

"Did you not have your phones on you? I tried calling a dozen times."

Mason shook his head. "We left them all charging in the truck."

"When did she get here?" asked Rogan.

"Hours ago."

He looked extremely uncomfortable at my answer. "And..."

"I'm not sure, really. She's been locked in that room ever since."

We waited until Desmond had entered his room, closing the door behind him. We could hear voices.

Murmurs...

Crying.

"Damn," said Rogan. "This is bad."

I followed them into their room, and we closed that door too. I began telling them everything that happened, as they peeled their wet clothes off.

"Holy shit," I said, pausing halfway through my story. "You guys are *wet*."

"The snow's blowing everywhere," said Mason. "It's making huge drifts."

"Yeah, but you look like you got into a water balloon fight!"

They had their shirts off now, and I stopped talking mid-sentence. They were glistening beautifully, all covered in sweat. It made every delicious ripple of muscle stand out even more starkly against their skin. I couldn't help but gawk at them.

"See anything you like?" Rogan chuckled.

They looked like a pair of bodybuilders, oiled up for a competition. Their wet skin, their soaked clothes — it all smelled like sex. Or maybe I just associated the smell with sex, because lately my sex life involved three sweaty guys taking turns on me.

"What else did she say?" asked Mason.

I shook my head, clearing it of a sex-soaked fog. They were peeling their jeans off now, but all that stuff would have to wait.

"She acted like she was supposed to be here," I said.

"Like she was still Desmond's girlfriend. She brought a suitcase with her. And... well..." I paused, feeling abruptly foolish. "She thought I was the maid."

Mason swore. Rogan shook his head. "What an asshole."

It surprised me a little, seeing them talk about her like this. Considering all the entries I'd read in her journal, that is.

"Was she always like this?"

"Yes and no," said Mason. "I mean, she was never this bossy, this insistent. She actually, well..."

"She used to be fun," Rogan finished for him. "For a while, anyway."

"That all changed after she worked at the company though," said Mason. "She wasn't qualified for the job, but of course her father gave it to her anyway. And rather than try to do it, she spent most of the time keeping an eye on Desmond."

"And on us too," said Rogan. "During the last year they were together, Emma was weirdly jealous. And then she got flighty. She started getting the urge to jump over the fence, and see if the grass was greener on the other side."

I nodded slowly. "And Desmond wouldn't go with her."

"Nope."

They were down to their underwear now. Rogan's red boxer-briefs showcased the two muscular legs leading up to his perfect, amazing ass. And Mason's pair barely contained the rounded swell of his big package.

"I call first shower," said Rogan.

Mason grunted. "Shit."

"You keep her company," smirked Rogan, grabbing a clean pile of clothes. "Don't worry, I'll be quick. And don't let—"

"I know, I know," said Mason. "I won't."

"Good."

He slipped out, and for a second or two we could hear voices through Desmond's door. They were louder now. Not exactly shouting, but not talking at a normal volume either.

The door closed, leaving Mason and I staring at each other in silence. Only he was naked. Mostly, anyway.

"So what are we going to do for the next ten minutes?" he joked.

"Well I'd have some fun ideas," I sighed, plopping down on the bed. "If your ex-girlfriend wasn't in the next room."

Mason's brow furrowed. "She's not my ex-girlfriend."

"You know what I mean."

It was a strange thing, jealousy. I'd spent the entire time at the cabin without a shred of it. And now suddenly... there it was.

"You shouldn't let Emma bother you," said Mason, sitting down next to me. "She's a non-factor. I don't know why she's here, but—"

"She's here to get Desmond back," I interjected. "Obviously."

"Yes, but he's over her. Totally and completely."

I'd been staring at the bedspread. I ventured a look upward. "You sure about that?"

"Absolutely."

He placed a comforting hand on my shoulder, and I leaned into him. Just then, the door opened and Desmond stepped into the room.

"Hey..."

He looked calm and cool. Not the least bit flustered.

"What's going on?" Mason asked.

"Not sure exactly," Desmond sighed, "but she's here. Somehow she thought it would be a good idea to 'surprise us'. Or more specifically, surprise me."

Mason grunted. "Mission accomplished."

"Yeah, unfortunately."

"You really had no idea?"

Desmond shook his head firmly. "I haven't talked to her once since she moved out west, you know that. Of course she's sent me a few random texts, telling me how great it was, maybe even fishing for a reply. And one presumably drunk text, telling me she missed me." He looked at me, his eyes open and honest. "But I never answered her. I deleted them all without responding."

Mason scratched at his square-stubbled jaw. "And she still *came?* Without an invite?"

"Took daddy's credit card and hopped on a plane," Desmond shrugged. "Literally showed up out of the clear blue sky."

"And where is she now?"

"In the kitchen, getting something to eat." He turned to face me. "She's *furious* that you're here," he said. "Especially with you sleeping in the master. She thinks—"

"I know what she thinks," I said glumly.

Desmond hesitated before continuing. "I assured her she was wrong about that," he went on. "I didn't exactly *want* to lie, but it wasn't like I could explain how—"

"Trust me," I said, holding a hand up. "I know."

All at once I felt terrible. Jealous. Totally out of place. They were feelings I hadn't felt the entire trip. With only two days left, I hated that I was feeling them now.

"I'm so sorry," I said, apologizing needlessly. "This is all my fault. I should never have—"

"Honey, don't."

"No seriously," I kept going. "I can gather my stuff and head to the airport right now. Grab an early flight back, so you guys don't have to—"

"Alyssa, *stop*."

Desmond's last word halted me, dead in my tracks. His voice was stern, almost angry. But not with me.

"If anyone's leaving, it's Emma," he said. "Not you. In fact, I'm putting *her* on a plane tomorrow, first thing in the morning."

The surge of adrenaline that had me practically vibrating on the edge of the bed abated a little. I tried forcing myself to calm down.

"So what happens now?" asked Mason.

"Well it's pretty late," explained Desmond. "And dark. I told her she could stay the night..."

Mason winced. Desmond went on.

"She insisted on being given the master."

"No problem," I jumped in. "I can totally—"

"I laughed in her face of course," Desmond continued. "I told her instead of that, she could sleep in my bed..."

I felt a sudden stab of jealousy. It twisted like a knife in my stomach, until—

"... while I take the couch."

Relief washed over me at first, followed by another bout of anger. Desmond shouldn't have to take the couch. I wanted him in *my* bed, his warm body snuggled beneath *my* sheets. As far as I was concerned, Emma could have the spare bedroom all to herself. In fact, she could fuck right off.

"Sorry if this is going to mess with our plans for tonight," Desmond apologized.

"Mess with them?" scoffed Mason. "It shatters them."

"Yeah," agreed Desmond. "But it's probably best to keep it low key. Get this night over with. Drive her to the airport in the morning."

"More like drag her there," sighed Mason. "Kicking and screaming."

Forty-Six

ALYSSA

It was the most awkward New Year's Eve of my life. Maybe even in recorded human history.

The five of us milled aimlessly around the cabin, which suddenly seemed ten times smaller than before. Emma ignored me completely. She wouldn't talk to me, look at me, or even acknowledge my presence.

And all that was just fine with me.

For the most part she huddled close to the fire, staring into the flames as if they held some kind of otherworldly answers. But when she wasn't doing that, she was following Desmond around like a little lost puppy. Hanging off his leg practically, while he mixed drinks and served up snacks.

I hated that part. Especially because he sometimes engaged her. He was polite as he needed to be, while trying to keep her comfortable. I could understand that part. That didn't mean I had to like it though.

The closer we got to midnight, the longer everything

seemed to drag on. I played chess with Mason. Backgammon with Rogan. I even cornered Desmond in the kitchen and kissed him quickly, while Emma was in the bathroom. It was a territorial thing, I knew. But I did it anyway. And the smile he gave me afterward made me feel a lot better about getting through the night.

Finally we watched the ball drop on television, while Desmond popped the top off a bottle of champagne. Together we toasted the new year, my glass touching everyone's but Emma's. After a round of awkward hugs and handshakes — during which Emma theatrically tried kissing every one of the guys on the mouth — we hit the lights and turned in.

I felt a thousand times more comfortable back in bed, once we'd all closed the doors to our respective rooms. I wasn't the slightest bit tired, really. But at least I didn't have to listen to Emma's fake laughter. Or pretend to ignore the obvious elephant in the room.

She feels ten times worse than you, you know.

I had to admit, that part made me feel somewhat guilty. In most respects, Emma was nothing more than an ex-girlfriend trying to rekindle an old flame. One she'd extinguished through her own selfish actions, of course. But even so, she was still just someone looking for love.

I could only imagine how she felt, seeing me here. Taking her spot on *this* trip. Basically replacing her, in just about every way.

I could forgive her for being angry with me. Even for hating me without even knowing me, or remembering me at all.

But she'd hurt Desmond. And that, I couldn't forgive.

I lay in bed for what seemed like an eternity, but was probably closer to forty-five minutes. It was cold with the door closed. Mason had been right about that on day one.

Screw this, I'm opening it.

I swung my legs off the bed and crept to the door, treading lightly so I wouldn't be heard. I didn't know why I was being so careful. It wasn't like I was doing anything wrong.

Maybe you should head into the living room. Climb all over Desmond.

Shit, *that* would be doing something wrong. Only it really wouldn't be, because it would feel nothing but right.

You could get him off that lumpy couch. Talk him into coming to bed with you...

Halfway to opening the door, I heard voices. A male voice... and a female one too. Both of them coming from the living room.

"Desmond... listen to me..."

I froze instantly, my heart sinking into my stomach.

Emma.

I not only opened my door, I pushed past it. Silently, on the balls of my feet, I made my way past her empty bedroom and down to the end of the hall.

Desmond was sprawled on the couch before the flicking fire. Emma knelt on the floor beside him. I could hear her murmuring to him. Pleading with him, as she reached out with one hand to touch his blanket-covered hip.

"Please, baby. Hear me out."

I was seething! Boiling over with anger. I wanted to rush in there and pull her away from Desmond.

"I would've been here sooner," Emma told him, not even trying to whisper. "If not for the snow. The blizzard shut *everything* down. Canceled flights all over the country for days on end."

She wasn't just touching him now, she was actually stroking him. Running her palm along the length of his thigh.

It was all I could do not to break her wrist.

"Stay with me," she said. "We need to talk. Send the others home, but stay with—"

Abruptly he took her wrist and pushed it forcefully away. Emma's chin dropped, her expression turning wounded.

"You're going home tomorrow," he said. "I told you, it's not even up for debate."

"But I just *got* here..."

"So? No one told you to come here, Emma. You left *months* ago. Not even a call, a text. Not even a letter saying goodbye."

She reached for him again. Again he batted her away.

"I couldn't do it," she sniffed. "When I made the decision to leave I was too emotional, too—"

"That decision was all yours, Emma. You made it and you'll have to live with it. And now you show up here? Starting trouble?" He shook his head. "No one invited you back into our lives."

I saw the glimmer of a tear rolling down her cheek. Whether it was real or fake, I couldn't tell.

"Baby *talk* to me," she pleaded. "Stay with me, an extra couple of days. I already told my father you wouldn't be in for the rest of the week. That he shouldn't expect you until *next* Monday."

I watched as Desmond bolted instantly upright on the couch. He moved so quickly she actually flinched.

"You actually *told* him that?"

She nodded happily.

"And your father said that was okay?"

"Yes," she said hopefully.

But Desmond was far from hopeful. "Why the hell would he let me do that?"

"Because I told him we're back together."

I had to pull back into the hallway a little, as Desmond shot to his feet. Emma leapt upward with him, still clinging to him pleadingly.

"Please, Desmond!" she gasped. "I'm back now, so you can have me again."

"But I don't *want* you."

"You will," she said coyly. "If you just give me a chance to—"

"You left, Emma! You moved to the other side of the country and abandoned everything here. And now you left again, because that's who you are. You're never happy. You can't comm—"

"And it's beautiful back there!" she exclaimed. "I only came back because I was lonely. But if I had *you* with me...

well, that would be different."

Desmond moved to the fireplace, and I saw her run to his side. Again he pulled away. As pathetic as the whole thing was, it made me vehemently angry. Angry that she thought she could come back to him so easily. As if this were truly the way the world worked.

"Stay with me after the others leave," she said again, "even if it's just for an extra day or so." She paused for a moment before continuing. "I can call my father, if you like. Make it so that Rogan and Mason can stay too, if that's what you want."

My fists clenched, involuntarily. I could feel my nails digging into my palms, almost to the point of drawing blood.

"Your *father*..." Desmond sneered. He hissed the word like a curse.

"My father will do whatever I tell him to do," Emma said, sounding rather pleased with herself. "I could have you fired tomorrow," she giggled. "And then you'd *have* to move away with me."

Desmond stiffened. He shoved her away with both hands.

"Emma, that's not funny."

She pulled her hair back over one ear, and I saw a wickedness in her expression. A vindictiveness that wasn't there only a moment ago.

"Who said it was funny?"

Emma whirled and stormed away, heading straight back towards the hall. Straight back towards me...

Shit!

There wasn't any time to get back to my room. It was too far. The door was still closed.

I steeled myself for the encounter. She was just three seconds from bumping into me. Two seconds...

Two hands shot out, grabbing me by the shoulders. I gasped at the sudden blur of motion, and suddenly I was standing in Rogan and Mason's bedroom, a hand clamped over my mouth.

"*Shhh!*"

They managed to close the door a split-second before Emma entered the hallway. The three of us stood there, utterly frozen, not daring to move until we heard the bedroom door across the hall slam shut again.

Then the hand relaxed, and I was left standing between two very warm, very welcoming bodies.

"Looks like your sleeping with us tonight," smiled Rogan, as he reached down to give my ass a promising squeeze.

Forty-Seven

ROGAN

"So you told her to fuck off home, right?"

Desmond stomped into the kitchen just as the waffle maker beeped and turned green. He tossed his keys on the table. Kicked off his boots.

"In no uncertain terms, yeah."

He'd done everything he'd promised us the night before. Not only had he gotten rid of Emma, he'd done it first thing in the morning. Before breakfast, even.

"I still can't believe she showed up."

"Oh I believe it," said Mason, flipping the last of the bacon. "After all, we're talking about *Emma*."

He was right, of course. When it came to surprises, Emma was the unrivaled queen. She'd prepared surprises for Desmond — both miraculously good and cataclysmically bad — that showed just how serious she was about keeping that title.

"How'd she end up taking it?"

"Not good," Desmond said, sinking into his chair.

I slid him a cup of coffee and clapped my hand on his shoulder. "Cheer up, bro. It's over now. She's someone else's problem now, wherever she goes to raise hell next."

"Yeah," he said, grabbing the sugar. "But that's also what I'm afraid of."

Emma. She'd been the queen of surprises, but also of being persistent. And the queen of other things too. Things I didn't even want to think about.

Like being vindictive...

"Hey..."

The three of us turned at the sound of Alyssa's voice. She stood in the kitchen archway, wearing her patchwork terrycloth bathrobe. Her hair stuck out in every possible direction.

"That's the most spectacular case of bed-head I've ever seen," I laughed.

"Thanks," she said wearily.

"Hey, no need to thank me," I laughed. "You definitely earned it." I began looking around. "In fact, where's my phone? I'm gonna need a picture of—"

"Is she gone?"

Mason was crunching down on a piece of bacon. Desmond was mid-gulp on his first sip of coffee.

"Oh yeah," I told her. "Ding dong, the witch is dead."

Alyssa's shoulders slumped visibly in relief. She let out such a stream of hot air it blew one of her cowlicks up and over the top of her head.

"Thank *God*."

"Shit yeah," Mason agreed. He dumped the bacon onto a drip-rack and flipped off the stove. "For a minute or two," he said, nodding toward Desmond, "I thought he was gonna actually get *back* with her."

Desmond scowled from over his coffee. "Bullshit," he snapped.

Mason and I both laughed. Not Alyssa though. Not this time.

My friend looked tired, and not just from taking an early run to the airport. He took another long pull of his coffee before continuing.

"I'm guessing you all heard our conversation last night?"

"Uh huh," I said. "All three of us."

We'd been right behind Alyssa in the hallway, listening to everything as it went down. There wasn't a moment I hadn't had faith in Desmond doing the right thing. But of course, I didn't want to tell *him* that.

"She's got some set of balls on her," Alyssa said, scooping some eggs on her plate. "I'll give her that."

Glancing sideways, she caught my eye. I smiled and gave her a fist bump.

God, she's so totally perfect.

Our bed-headed beauty had spent the night beneath our blankets, cuddled between us in nothing more than her tiny underwear. Somehow though, Mason and I had controlled ourselves. We hadn't made love to her, hadn't even made *out* with her, as much as we'd wanted to.

But I grinded on her so hard my erection took *hours* to subside.

I'd spent those hours thinking about her, though. Wondering how amazing it would be to keep going with what we had, even after we'd gotten back. It was something I knew I desperately wanted. I only hoped that once we'd returned to Florida and gotten back into our old routines, that Alyssa would feel the same way.

"It's crazy that she'd think to just fly out here at the last minute," said Mason. "And expect well... you know."

"That's Emma for you," said Desmond, shaking his head. "Maybe she'll learn, though. Maybe this'll be the wake up call she needed."

I nodded in mock agreement, wanting to believe it. But I wasn't sure I did.

"Let's forget about her," said Desmond abruptly. "We've got one day left — today. Let's enjoy it. Let's ride out the last of our vacation together, before work rears it's ugly head again."

"Besides," shrugged Alyssa. "It's an all new year." She held up an overcooked piece of bacon. "Here's to new things," she said, her eyes shining. "And new beginnings."

We each grabbed some bacon and toasted her in turn. My piece was so overcooked, it actually shattered on impact.

"Are you *ever* going to learn to cook properly?" Desmond snapped, whirling on Mason.

"Fuck no," Mason laughed.

Forty-Eight

ALYSSA

We shook off the bad mojo of Emma's impromptu visit, and really made our last day count. Since we still had passes, we skied a little. Had dinner and drinks. Said goodbye to the quaint little town, and came home to take down all the Christmas decorations and pack up the cabin.

Together the guys dragged our tree outside, into a cute little corner of the yard. Desmond vowed to plant it in the fall, when he came back to winterize the cabin. Or maybe even take a quick trip up in the spring, and do it then.

Either way we'd have something to commemorate our time here. The tree would grow, and it could be decorated year after year. A lifelong reminder of our first — and hopefully not our last — Christmas, here at the cabin.

Exactly what are you doing, Alyssa?

The voice popped into my head whenever I thought this way. Whenever I dared think that what the four of us currently had could actually stand the test of time.

You know it can't last, right?

I hated this pessimistic voice. I was generally an optimistic person. Yet I knew my heart; once we got back to Florida, everything would be different. Once we were all back in our own apartments, living our normal, everyday lives, it would be more likely that we'd grow apart rather than stick together.

More than anything, I realized I wanted to continue to see the guys. And not just one of them, but all three. It seemed crazy to think I could settle for one, or even two, when I was so attached to the three of them as a trio. Their group dynamic. The camaraderie of their friendship, of which I now considered myself fully a part of.

For me, it was an all or nothing deal. I couldn't imagine what it would be like, dating one of the guys and having to look at the other two. Having to watch them date other women. Get girlfriends of their own. Fall in love...

Do you love them?

It was a crazy question. One I'd been putting off the entire second half of our trip. We'd started purely on sexual ground, doing things we all knew were naughty but fun. Yet as the sex only got better? The attachments began. The feelings of closeness and kinship. The emotional connections that came along with the physical ones.

I'd learned so much about the guys that I *never* would've found out while simply working alongside them. I knew Desmond's dreams of owning his own construction company. I knew Rogan's sense of humor came from his fun-loving dad. I knew Mason secretly wanted to know his half-sisters, and possibly even reconcile with his father, too. He just didn't know how to go about doing that. And I desperately wanted to help him.

You're avoiding the question, Alyssa.

Yes, I loved them. And it felt so good to say it! Even just to myself, even internally, in the secret chambers of the back of my mind.

I loved them more than any guy I'd ever dated, individually and as a trio as well. Because as cool and amazing as each of the men were, there was a whole new level of awesomeness that came with the three of them being together.

That sounds greedy as fuck.

"Yeah," I said out loud, packing the last of my suitcase. "It sure does."

I pulled on the zipper. Yanked it hard, until it finally sealed every last bit of my dirty laundry away for the trip home.

Then I told the voice in my head to shut the hell up.

Forty-Nine

ALYSSA

"You know we *could* blindfold you again," suggested Rogan. "Spread you out before the fire and have you take guesses."

"Oh?" I replied. "Just like the kissing contest?"

"Sort of..." he said slyly. "But a different *kind* of kissing."

I stared into the fireplace, watching the flames. Feeling the heat wash over my nearly naked body, as I paraded before the guys in my last clean thong.

"Tempting, but no," I said, pushing the two of them backward on the couch. "I promised my boys a round of fireside blowjobs." Looking over my shoulder, I gave Desmond a devilish wink. "And a promise is a promise."

Mason and Rogan had their boxers down in seconds, kicking them off while I dropped to my knees. I crawled over, turning my back to the fire. The flames felt good on my ass as I took each of them in my hand.

"I want you both to come in my mouth," I instructed, licking Rogan up and down while staring at Mason. "And he's going to watch."

I jerked my chin toward Desmond, relaxing in the big leather chair beside us. He looked buzzed and content, the last of our beers dangling from between his fingers.

"I'll do him last," I winked. "I'll make it *good*."

Rogan groaned as I took him to the root. Then I switched to Mason. Back and forth, I went on for a full two minutes. Taking each of them down my throat. Getting them all hard and glistening and sloppy wet.

"I'm going to *swallow* you," I breathed huskily. "Every bit. Every drop." I flipped my hair back and opened my mouth. With everyone watching, I pointed sluttily to the flat of my hot, wet tongue.

"I want it right. Fucking. Here."

The two men on the couch throbbed hard, swelling even bigger in my two eager fists. I'd been looking forward to this for days. I'd wanted to do this for them... *to* them... since before I even made the promise.

Ohhh, shit yes.

It was even hotter than I thought it would be.

I'd imagined our last night here would be hotter than hell, but I wanted to make it extra memorable. I wanted my guys to relax. To reward them for inviting me on such an amazing trip by bringing them off in my mouth, one by one.

Most of all I wanted them to *enjoy* it. To worry about only their own pleasures, as I became their hot little toy again.

I wanted to take the edge of each of them; to drink them down until the hot musk of their combined seed was sizzling away, deep in my belly.

And then I wanted to lay back and get *destroyed.*

"Mmmmm..."

I moaned and I groaned. Waved my thong-covered ass enticingly at Desmond, as I sucked his friends slowly and sensually, rather than hard and fast. I wanted to take my *time* with them. To forever sear this night into each of their brains, so that no matter what life threw our way back in Florida, we'd always have *this*.

It felt incredibly sexy, rotating between them. Servicing them from my knees. I thought back to our first time together, where they were so gentle and patient with me. To our kissing contest, and how steamy and sensuous the whole thing had been.

I wanted them to remember this night, but I wanted them to remember *me*. Two weeks ago we'd been strangers. Now were good friends. Passionate lovers.

And so *very* much more.

Rogan came first, firing an impressive amount of his delicious seed straight down my throat. After pumping him dry I went at Mason with a vengeance, until he too was ready to explode.

I waited until he was past the point of no return, then pulled him abruptly from my mouth. Shifting my gaze, I made direct eye contact with Desmond. I saw his expression go drunk with lust, as he watched me jerk his friend the rest of the way off, straight onto the flat of my tongue.

"UNGHHH!"

Mason's ass left the couch as he blasted off, filling my mouth. I continued without looking away, without even wincing as the tremendous head twitched and pumped against my tongue. As promised, I took every drop he had. I held it there in my mouth for a moment, then swallowed it all down while still eye-fucking Desmond.

Then, unable to take it anymore, he rushed me.

Ohhhh YES.

His hands felt magnificent on my body as he spun me around. He practically tore my thong in half! I heard it snap in his big fist as he yanked his arm backwards, utterly destroying the thin, flimsy fabric.

He entered me in one glorious, savage thrust, filling me all the way up. I grunted happily as he bounced off my body and rammed himself straight back inside.

God...

Over and over he kept nailing me, hard and fast and deep. Desmond's hands wound themselves into my hair. He rolled them into fists and jerked my head unapologetically back, forcing my chin upward.

"Ohhhh!"

Then he was jackhammering me from behind, sawing into me again and again. Grunting all kinds of nasty things into my ear, like telling me how tight and wet my pussy felt, and how it *begged* him to be used the whole time I was blowing his friends.

Oh my GOD...

I nearly cried it all felt so good.

The others watched from the couch, their hard bodies still making my mouth water as I screwed the alpha of their little group. As friends and coworkers they'd always been equal, always been on the same ground. But when it came to this...

Well, Desmond was clearly in control.

I whimpered and cried as he screwed me, bucking my ass back against him nonetheless. And then I was coming. Exploding from the inside out, my eyes literally crossing until my vision doubled and I could see *four* men on the couch, stroking themselves back to life. Getting themselves hard again and ready for me, the moment their friend was done punishing my body for all the teasing I'd done.

OHHhhHHhhHHH...

My climax was never-ending. It spun out in waves of the purest rapture, each one more powerful than the last. Somewhere behind me was the pain of Desmond pulling my hair with one great hand. Squeezing the supple flesh of my ass between the fingers of his other. I cried out again and again, but my cries were always in pleasure. The pain was just the very edge. The sharp, jagged tip of something much bigger and more important, as I exploded again and again all over Desmond's hard, thrusting manhood.

I was half-delirious when he finally exploded. Still coming down from the greatest orgasm of my life, when I felt him throbbing and pumping and filling me from within.

H—Holy—

He was screaming my name. Roaring like a lion as he

shoved himself all the way home, splashing the insides of my womb with his warm, wonderful seed.

Holy shit...

I writhed beneath him, clawing at the blankets. Screaming every bit as loudly, grunting and gasping at the pleasure he was taking in ravaging my body. He collapsed on top of me, virtually crushing me beneath his great weight. Locking his arms to give me just enough breathing room... while keeping his warm, naked skin pressed tightly against mine.

Still inside me, his lips found the outer edge of my ear. And then he whispered — so low it was just between us — and his whisper gave me a shiver of goosebumps from head to toe:

"I think I'm in *love* with you..."

Fifty

ALYSSA

I'd found my apartment staring back at me, exactly the way I'd left it.

Even so, it looked totally foreign somehow. Like everything was somehow different. Yet it was the same basic layout I'd been living with the past two years. There was the couch I sat in, watching movies alone. The refrigerator I'd cleaned out just before leaving, getting rid of anything perishable that wouldn't last more than two weeks.

Last night I'd dragged my suitcase into the back room, and flopped down on my immaculately-made bed. Shit, it all seemed such a lifetime ago. Being here. Waking up to *this* alarm clock. Looking up at *this* ceiling...

And now it was the following morning. And instead of waking up to breakfast with the guys... I was sitting alone in my office, staring at a screen again.

Fuck my life.

Coming back from vacation on a Friday was the worst

of all possible choices — a really dick move I'd pulled on myself. While the rest of the office would be goofing off and winding their week down, I'd be catching up on a thousand emails. Fixing a hundred problems all at once, or at least trying to put enough band-aids on them to get me through the weekend.

But at least I'd be seeing the guys again.

I'd already run into Mason, on my way in. We'd shared a secret smile, and he'd given me a wink that melted my heart.

Yeah, I could live with a day of craziness if it meant seeing my three beautiful coworkers again. Men who weren't just coworkers anymore but who were now my lovers... and possibly even more.

It's only been a day.

The thought made me laugh. I'd kissed the guys goodbye just yesterday, after our relatively smooth flight home. And yet I already missed them. I'd spent a lonely night in my apartment, without anyone to talk to. Slept through the night, without one or more of them climbing into my bed.

This was a whole new world now, for all of us. The same job with the same people. The same duties and tasks. Only *we'd* changed. The dynamic between us, forever altered, by our time away.

And then there were Desmond's words...

I think I'm in love with you.

He could've said them in the heat of passion, of course. But I didn't think so. If anything, the fact that he said them afterwards meant even more to me. Because right at that time, we were as physically and emotionally close as two people could be.

As happy as these thoughts were, I tried putting them out of my head for a little bit. There was so much to do. So much to catch up on.

I skipped lunch and signed off on a record number of plan addendums. I sent out so many project updates my head started spinning. I attributed part of my success to keeping my office door closed, to ward off the inevitable dozen or more people who would wander in, smile cleverly, and ask how my 'holiday vacation with the guys' had gone. Slowly though, I got caught up.

It was almost five when my door opened, without so much as a knock. Rogan slipped in. I smiled up at him happily… but the look of concern on his face erased that smile immediately.

"What's wrong?"

He squinted down at me for a moment, then back through the doorway. Closing it behind him, he tilted his head.

"You really don't know?"

That cold, uneasy feeling of *not* knowing something stole over me. Something big.

"No, what?"

Rogan swallowed before continuing. "It's Emma."

The feeling was even colder. And now I was sinking…

"What about her?"

Sinking fast.

"She's here."

I blinked a few times rapidly before standing up. "*Here?*" I asked stupidly. "As in here in the office, or—"

"She's not only here in the office," Rogan replied, "she's *back*. Working for Green Valley, that is. Her father gave her her old job back."

All of a sudden my legs felt like jelly. I slumped back down, into my chair.

"She's got an *office* now, too," said Rogan. "And guess where it is?"

I didn't have to guess. I already knew.

"Right by Desmond's desk?"

"Right *next* to Desmond's desk," he confirmed. "Only Desmond hasn't even been at his desk. He's been out in the field all day."

I let out a short laugh. "Wouldn't you be, if you were him?"

"Yes, but—"

"Yes but nothing," I said. "He's obviously avoiding her. Can't say I blame him, either. Especially the way—"

"No, it's not that," Rogan cut in. "Apparently she's got additional duties now. Besides not doing the job she already doesn't do, the old man delegated the coordination of site inspections."

My brow furrowed. It didn't make sense. "She'll screw that up royally."

"Of course," Rogan agreed. "But she *asked* for it. And whatever Emma asks for, daddy gives her."

Slowly I was coming around. Starting to understand.

"She sent Desmond away today, didn't she?"

Rogan nodded, his look still grave.

"Well... shit."

"And who knows what else she'll do," he went on. "Remember the last time she worked here, when her father put her in charge of the work trucks? In two months none of them had oil changes and she'd let all the insurance lapse."

I shook my head in disbelief. "How'd Desmond date this girl for so long?" I marveled. "And how the hell did the three of you put up with—"

BZZZZZT.

Our phones buzzed, at exactly the same time. We both looked down at our four-way group chat, where there was a new message from Desmond.

Drinks tonight.

It was a statement, not a question.

Fifty-One

ALYSSA

It turned out the situation with Emma wasn't as bad as Rogan and I originally thought.

Actually, it was *worse*.

"So she sent you *away?*" Mason asked in astonishment. "Just because you wouldn't have *coffee* with her?"

"All day," Desmond nodded. "I spent the last nine hours driving to six different jobs. I ran supplies for three of them, everything from drywall to joist hangers to a hot water heater coil."

He shook his head as he drained the rest of his beer. Before he could set down the empty mug, Rogan was already pouring it full again.

"I picked up finish nails today, bro," he sighed angrily. "Fucking *finish nails.*"

We learned that a lot of things had happened while we were away. Most notably of course, that Emma's father had provided a plane ticket so she could return to Florida 'for good'. He'd also set her up in a position of authority within the company that was well beyond the scope of her abilities. Not to mention way past her ability to cope with rejection.

"So what are you going to do when she wants coffee on Monday?" I asked.

"I'm going to have coffee with her," said Desmond. "Then the two of us will sit down, and I'll lay everything out for her in black and white."

"Umm... wanna lay it out for us, first?" joked Mason.

Desmond went on, speaking loud enough to be heard over the bar noise. We'd driven a bit further than normal, to a place out of town. Well away from the office, and whatever prying eyes might still be lingering.

"She's going to have to get over it," he eventually finished. "I'm way past the point of playing these high school games."

"And what if she doesn't?" I asked hesitantly.

"Doesn't what?"

"Get over it."

Desmond grunted and gripped his mug a little bit tighter. Mason took the opportunity to grab the pitcher of beer and top the rest of us off.

"She'll have to," he said again. "Or I'll go to the old man and have a talk with him myself."

Rogan raised an eyebrow. "You'll go and talk to the boss?" he winced. "About his *daughter?*"

"Yeah."

He and Mason exchanged concerned glances. "That didn't quite work out for you the last time you tried it."

"Yes, well hopefully he's more reasonable this time," Desmond replied. "Besides, he's gotta know by now his daughter is nothing but trouble."

"Flighty? Yes," I said. "Maybe even a bit incompetent. But trouble?" I shook my head. "No parent wants to admit that his kid is trouble."

We talked it over some more, going over our options. Creating contingency plans for what might or could happen. Then, after finishing our second pitcher, we were back out in the parking lot. Climbing into the smooth leather seats of Mason's pristine German car, for the ride back to the office to pick up our own vehicles.

"So what's the plan for tonight?" asked Rogan.

"Laundry," Desmond grumbled. "Laundry, laundry, and more laundry."

"You mean you don't send it out?" asked Rogan.

"You *do?*"

"Oh you gotta send it out," laughed Mason. "It's the best thing in the world! They wash it. They fold it. They do everything except put it away." He shook his head as he pulled smoothly onto the highway. "You're a sucker if you don't send it ou—"

"Bring it to my place."

Desmond spun from his place in the passenger seat to look back at me.

"Really?"

I nodded quickly. "I've got one of those stacked washer-dryers in my apartment. It's not the best model in the world, but it works." I shrugged. "We could do it there."

"I've got a lot of laundry," he warned. "It'll probably take all night."

I looked back into those blue eyes and smiled. "I've got all night."

We'd already decided beforehand to spend the evening together. The four of us, cementing the bond right here that we'd made all the way up in Vermont.

"Besides," I went on, "it felt so weird sleeping alone in my place last night." I looked from one guy to the next, drinking them in. "It doesn't even feel like home right now. To be honest, I sort of, well... I need *memories* of you there."

I blushed, glancing at all three of them. "If that makes any sense."

Rogan's ensuing smile was zero business, all pleasure. "What kind of memories are we talking about here?"

"*That* kind," I giggled. "Plus the other ones too. All memories, really," I said. "I just— I just want to..."

"*Be* with us?" asked Desmond.

"Yes."

He nodded, and the rest of them followed suit. I could feel the excitement returning. The same happiness I associated with being back at the cabin.

Desmond reached over the seat, gently brushing the side of my cheek with his hand.

"I think we all feel the same way."

The Christmas Toy - Krista Wolf

Fifty-Two

ALYSSA

Having the guys in my apartment was like bringing them into that last part of my world. A connection between the fantasy of Vermont and the reality of home, and every minute that went by only solidified that bond.

We sent out for pizza, and I showed them around. It was almost surreal, seeing them standing there in my foyer, relaxing on my couch. Watching them settle into the chairs around my kitchen table, passing each other my little container of crushed red pepper while talking and laughing and falling right back into our old routine.

We discussed the situation with Emma a bit more, but not for very long. She'd dominated our thoughts far too long to begin with. In the cabin there were memories of her, and that was understandable. But right here, right now, she just didn't belong.

Together we steered the conversation down more constructive avenues, talking about everything from work to family and more. Rogan had been given two more design projects — one of which I'd be working with him on. He planned on visiting his sisters and nieces next week, to do the whole 'post Christmas' thing up in the panhandle.

Mason had a conference on Monday and would be gone for several days — a last-minute trip added to his schedule while we were away. And Desmond's own work was still piling up, because he hadn't been back behind his desk yet.

We rented a movie but hardly watched it. Lounged around on my living room furniture, until Mason accidentally knocked over his beer, spilling it over my carpet.

"We making memories yet?" Rogan laughed.

"Some, yeah," I smiled, as I snuggled into his arms. "Not the *best* kind, though. Not yet."

I made my way around the room as the night went on, wrapping myself around each of them. They took turns holding me tight, nuzzling and kissing me, exactly the way they had in the cabin.

Only this was *here*. And for me, that was important.

As the night wound down we dimmed the lights and the fireworks began all over again. I took them all exactly where I wanted them, right there on the living room floor. There wasn't a fireplace. We didn't have the warm, blinking lights of a fragrant Christmas tree. But even without those things, it felt as it did before. Every kiss, every touch — every time one of them pinned my legs back over his shoulders, causing me to gasp as he took me deep...

It finally felt like home.

I had them all over the house too, just for good measure. Invited them to take me anywhere and everywhere they wanted, just to break things in. I clawed the cushions as Desmond screwed me deep into the couch. Held on for dear life while Mason took me on the kitchen table, right next to the empty pizza boxes.

Rogan bent me over the drafting table in my office, wrapping one corded arm tightly around my waist as he screwed me from behind. We ended up writhing against the wall, his entire length jammed so deep he had to cover my mouth with one hand to prevent me from screaming...

In the end though, I dragged them all back into my bedroom. One by one I pushed them onto their backs and had my way with them, impaling myself on each of my beautiful lovers and riding them until I'd had my fill.

And oh... how I was *filled*.

It wasn't until the wee hours of the morning that I was finally satisfied, and even then I felt like I could go for more. But the guys were spent. They lay next to me in various states of arousal, tracing my body with their fingertips, kissing me softly the way lovers do.

This is perfect.

I nursed their eager mouths against my warm breasts. Twisted and writhed, until I was cuddling their bodies with mine. I felt like a queen or an empress, enveloped by her loving harem. Surrounded by heated flesh. Protected in every way, by strength and stamina and glorious acres of hard, quivering muscle.

This is heaven.

I was having my cake and eating it too. Dragging every girl's deepest one-time fantasy from the most perverted recesses of my mind, and stretching it into a full-blown relationship with three incredible guys.

I wanted nothing more than to be the center of their world. And I wanted to be theirs, wholly and completely. Devoted to their own dreams, their own happiness. Fulfilling their every wish, their every whim.

For a long time I stared upward and outward, through the window of my apartment and into the hazy night sky. I had everything I'd ever wanted. From my standpoint, everything in the world was finally perfect...

It wasn't until the next week that it all went to shit.

Fifty-Three

MASON

"What do you mean they took his *desk?*"

We were in Rogan's office, with the door uncharacteristically closed. For once the look on my friend's face was serious. Alyssa was choking back tears... or maybe it was anger. I couldn't tell which.

"He's been in the field all week," explained Rogan. "And then the old man called him into the office this morning. Something about too many cooks, not enough soup."

"No," Alyssa spat. "It was *way* stupider than that."

"Whatever," Rogan said, brushing it off. "Either way, they told him there were too many managers working things from the office, and not enough people hands-on. They gave him his old truck and put him back on crews again." He looked at the floor. "Permanently."

My stomach lurched. Desmond had spent a long time working his way into the office. Besides, it wasn't just a seniority thing. When it came to construction he had more in-depth knowledge than every other project manager.

Which could only mean one thing...

"Emma."

I grunted the word. The others nodded.

"What a vindictive bitch," I seethed. "Just because of what he said on Monday?"

"And Tuesday," said Alyssa. "And Wednesday..."

I'd been away all week. Holed up in a financial conference down in Miami; three days of crunching numbers and shaking hands with people I'd rather not know. At least the food had been good, even if I couldn't see the nightlife. I'd barely had time to do anything but shuttle back and forth between meetings and the hotel.

"Where is he now?"

"Not sure," said Rogan. "I tried calling him. She has too."

Alyssa stood across from us, arms folded, her face drawn with worry. Even upset she looked stunningly beautiful. But the last thing I wanted was to see her upset.

"Someone's gotta talk to the old man," I said. "He needs to know what she's doing."

"He *does* know," said Rogan. "And that's the problem."

God, the whole thing was such bullshit! We worked for a man who would literally drive his company into the ground if his daughter suggested it. When it came to her, there was no talking to him. Desmond had learned that the last time, trying to smooth things over after the two of them had broken up.

"Look, he's going to back her," said Rogan. "No matter what we do or say, he'll stand behind Emma. Even worse, he'll make Desmond out to be the belligerent asshole. The insubordinate ex-boyfriend who's 'just pissed' that his ex-girlfriend happens to be working in the office again."

Crap. He was totally right.

"She's already said something to that effect," choked Alyssa. "Something about 'my father said if we can't play nice then one of us has to leave'."

I growled. Literally growled. "And we can all guess who that someone will be, too."

"Uh huh."

I reached up with one hand, squeezing my temples as if it would somehow end my suddenly raging headache. It didn't even come close.

"You know, even with Desmond out of the office this won't be the end of it," I said. "She feels slighted by all of us somehow. And every day she sees us, it'll be a reminder of that."

Mason nodded. Alyssa looked concerned.

"How long before some of our better projects start getting reassigned?" I asked sharply. "Before she's screwing us all over, in any way she can?"

It was an unsettling thought. I already knew Monday's conversation between Desmond and Emma had devolved quickly, leaving her hurt and upset. He'd even tried consoling her, but that only made it worse.

But I could totally see Emma doing something like

this. Not the Emma we knew a long time ago, but the Emma who'd come back from wherever she'd run off to?

That was an entirely different person.

"Something has to happen," Rogan agreed, "before she blows everything up. She'll out us in front of the whole office, all four of us. She won't even think twice."

"If she outs us, she outs herself," I pointed out. "And in front of her father..."

"We need to find Desmond," Alyssa pleaded. "He stormed out of here so fast, I can't even imagine—"

My phone rang, and my friend's name appeared on screen. I placed it in the middle of my desk and pressed the speaker button.

"Buddy where are you?" I asked for all of us.

"Home."

Desmond's voice came through loud and clear. It was a single terrifying word, with a seething edge to it.

"Why?" asked Alyssa, after a moment of silence.

"Why?" he laughed cynically. "Because I don't work there anymore, that's why."

A cold chill stole over me, as my hands screwed into fists. *Goddammit.*

"You got *fired?*" Rogan asked incredulously. It was unfathomable. Unconceivable.

"No, not fired," Desmond said plainly. "I *quit.*"

Fifty-Four

ALYSSA

I spent the rest of the day seething, boiling over with rage. Trying my best to listen to the story Desmond told of his meeting with our boss, and how things had gone almost instantly south.

Desmond wasn't willing to take a demotion, and not one of us could blame him. At first he took the high road, trying to talk sense into our boss without mentioning Emma at all. He explained how he was ten times more valuable in the office than running errands out in the field. That he'd put in long years on dozens of crews, and cited everything he'd done for Green Valley since the day he was hired.

But the old man wasn't having any of it.

If our boss was anything at all, it was unreasonably stubborn. On top of that he was fiercely overprotective when it came to his daughter, and had zero good things to say about her 'troublemaker' of an ex-boyfriend.

In short, Desmond's battle had been uphill the whole

time. He'd lost before it had even begun.

Rogan and Mason had gone home already. Something about a plan Desmond had, or some kind of a 'next step'. But I knew enough to realize nothing would work here. Not in this office. Not after what happened.

Part of me wanted to go straight to the old man. To sit him the hell down and talk some sense into him. He needed to realize Desmond was one of the best people he had. And that he was throwing that asset away over nothing more than his bratty daughter's vendetta against an ex-boyfriend's rejection.

But then Emma walked past my window.

She smiled at me — the bitch actually *smiled* at me! And along with that, an accompanying wave.

Holy SHIT!

I was up in an instant. My hands were balled into fists, and both those fists wanted to find new homes in Emma's smug, sneering face.

Before I did though... I grabbed something from the drawer of my desk.

I flung open my door, and stepped briskly out onto the main floor. Emma noticed me immediately. The look of smug satisfaction melted a little as she realized she might've pushed me too far. That I might actually revel in the satisfaction of kicking her ass... in front of twenty or thirty of our closest co-workers.

I saw her rush into her office and quickly attempt to close the door. I was faster, though. I wedged my foot in first, then pushed my way in.

"Are you out of your goddamn *mind?*" I swore, as the door swung shut behind me.

Well... so much for reasoning with her.

Emma stood with her hands on her hips, her expression completely indignant. For a split second I was sure she was going to yell for security. But then we locked eyes... and I saw her pride get in the way.

"Do you *really* want to do this?" she challenged, folding her arms.

"How could you do this to him!" I shouted. "After everything the two of you have been through, *this* is the way you—"

"Oh, stop it!"

She leaned back against her desk, looking more sure of herself than she actually was. Her eyes were cold now. Calculating.

"Are you seriously going to lecture *me?*" Emma sneered. "You, the girl who jumped right into my shoes the moment I took them off?"

"You were the one who took them off," I pointed out.

"And you were willing to slide right in," she scoffed. "Literally."

Her eyes blazed, but so did mine. There was no use denying or sugarcoating anything. We both knew where we stood.

"That's fine," I said. "The jealousy I understand. Hate me all you want to. But Desmond—"

"—is a grown man who can fight his own battles,"

Emma countered. "Does he really need his latest slut to speak up for him? Because the Desmond I knew—"

I trashed her desk. It happened in an instant, without any thought or pretense. One second I was rushing forward, ready to rip her to shreds. The next... just about everything on her desk was violently scattered across the floor.

Emma looked down at the mound of paper, work supplies, pens and everything else. I'd spared her laptop. Probably only because it was plugged in.

"You'll be gone for this," she said acidly.

"Oh yeah?" I sneered. "Are you gonna tell *daddy* on me?"

That struck a nerve. I saw her entire complexion go instantly red.

"Maybe daddy needs to know exactly why his best contractor just resigned. Did you tell him? Does he know?"

I stepped into her, but the dangerous edge to my anger was gone. It didn't stop the intimidation factor, though.

"Did you tell him about Rogan?" I asked. "And about Mason too? Does your father know all the twisted little things you *did* with them? And how it made you so petty and vindictive?"

She backed up, but there was nowhere to go. Emma was against the wall now. Looking out through the glass enclosure at the front of her office, possibly for help.

"You're not angry at me for doing the same things you did," I snarled. "You're only bitter from the rejection."

She blinked. The truth hurt.

"Maybe daddy needs to know his business is being held hostage by some oversexed, lovesick brat?"

Emma swallowed hard and seemed to regain some of her composure. "Oversexed?" she scoffed. "You're one to talk! Try going anywhere near my father's office and I'll tell him *exactly* what you're doing."

"I'll just deny everything," I shrugged, with a little laugh. "Then I'll go to HR. Report you for harassment."

She looked utterly confused now. Like she was so spoiled, the whole thing never occurred to her.

"Of course, *you* won't be able to deny the same thing," I went on. "And I hate to say it, but your father will totally believe me."

Emma's face curled into a smirk of denial. "Yeah. Sure."

"Especially when I show him *this*."

Slowly I reached behind me... and pulled out her journal. She didn't recognize the book immediately. But the very second she did, her heart sank.

Damn... I thought to myself.

It was a dirty thing to do. Taking the journal from the cabin and packing it away. Keeping it safe at the office, for the moment trouble with Emma might eventually start. I really didn't *want* to pull it out, or use it, or God forbid go through the awkward charade of showing it to her father. In all honesty, I wasn't even sure I could do something like that to a person.

But Emma didn't know that.

"You... you took my—"

"Yes."

"BITCH!"

"Alright," I smiled. "I'll take that one."

Emma's expression was half rage, half just-got-gut-punched. I tucked the journal away and moved back toward the door.

"You know what to do," I said evenly. "You tell your father the whole thing with Desmond was just a mistake. You put him back on his existing work, and you stop messing with his job."

She took a slow step forward, being careful not to slip on the fallen paperwork. "And then you'll give me back my journal?"

"Sure," I told her. "And then we all play nice together. Especially you, because in the back of your mind, you'd know it would've taken me all of three minutes to snap *photos* of every page of this journal." I tilted my head. "Wouldn't it?"

Her shoulders slumped, as did the rest of her body. Her expression was different now. I could see the defeat in her eyes.

"Look, this is all pretty easy," I said. "All you have to do is nothing..." I shrugged. "And then nothing happens."

I turned to leave, before things went further south. I'd had my say. Anything else would be counterproductive. Either Emma would do the right thing, or she'd—

"Okay..."

Hesitantly I looked back. Her arms were crossed again.

"I'll tell my father. I'll leave him alone."

The words sank in. I could see she meant them, as she shrugged one shoulder.

"I should probably thank you anyway," she said snidely, the smirk returning to her face. "For reminding me my new life was better. That I should have never come back here, trying to make the same stupid mistake."

I waited until I got to the doorway before replying. "Actually I should be the one thanking you," I said, with a mocking, sugary sweetness. "If it weren't for me finding your journal... none of this would've ever happened."

Fifty-Five

ALYSSA

"So?" I asked excitedly. "Which do you want first?"

I'd gotten to Desmond's apartment in record time. Flying happily along on the high of everything that had just happened. I found the boys gathered around the table in his kitchen. Staring down at his laptop, and a bunch of other stuff as well.

I expected them to look forlorn. Bitter and angry at Desmond's departure. Instead, they actually seemed excited about something. And this was even *before* I made my announcement.

"Good news or better news..." Rogan repeated. "Hmm... that's a tough one." He turned to Desmond. "I don't know, man. Which do we want first?"

"Tell us the good news," said Mason.

"The good news is that Emma won't be bothering us anymore," I smiled happily. I made sure to catch Desmond's gaze. "*Any* of us."

"Shit. That *is* good news," Rogan swore. "You're telling us there's better news than tha—"

"And Desmond has his job back."

All three of them went silent, as I leaned back with a satisfied grin. Only they didn't seem surprised. They didn't even seem excited.

"Did you hear what I said?" I blinked. "Emma's going to talk to her father. She's promised to take back everything she's ever told him about you."

Desmond nodded slowly. "That's pretty cool, actually."

I squinted back at him in confusion. "Are you not getting this?" I asked. "You've got your *job* back! You won't be in the field anymore, you'll be back in your office and—"

"But I don't want my job back."

Now it was my turn to sit there in astonishment. The kitchen went so silent, I could hear the ticking of Desmond's plastic wall clock.

"I resigned, Alyssa. The old man didn't fire me."

"Yes, but you quit because of Emma!"

My big beautiful boyfriend shrugged his massive shoulders halfway. "Yeah, she was a catalyst. Or rather, maybe you could call her the straw that broke the camel's back."

"But you can come back to GVB," I said. "From what she hinted, Emma's probably leaving anyway. Why leave Green Valley Builders after you've worked so hard to—"

"Because of this," said Desmond, turning his laptop around.

I stared down at his computer. Scattered across the screen were a jumble of numbers, all with dollar signs attached to them. A huge spreadsheet, with rows and columns and totals.

"I–I don't get it."

"I'm going into business for myself," said Desmond, as Mason cleared his throat. "No, scratch that. *We're* going into business for *ourselves.*"

I looked again at the spreadsheet. I saw supply lists. Permit costs. Financing estimates, and loan percentages. There were windows open behind the spreadsheet, on real estate sites. They matched some of the printouts already on the table.

"I'm done working for other people," said Desmond. "I've been doing it for years and I've already got all the knowledge. I can act as my own general contractor, from start to finish. Develop properties of my own, from the ground up."

My mind spun. This wasn't what I expected at all! And it all sounded so good. Maybe too good.

"Do you think you're ready for all that?"

"Hell yeah he's ready," said Rogan. "He's been ready for years, he just didn't know it. And now he's got backing. Now he's got help." He elbowed Mason, who grunted his agreement.

"I've got savings," said Desmond. "Pretty substantial savings, actually."

"So do I," said Mason. "So does Rogan."

"I thought about flipping first," Desmond went on. "Buying some distressed properties and fixing them up. But you know what? I'd rather *build*. I've been working at GVB long enough to have all the contacts I'd ever need. I have the property auction schedules. I know where to get the land, and where to buy the materials. Rogan can do the design, file the plans, get the permits..."

"Mason does the financing," Rogan went on. "He gets us the builder's loans. He deals with payroll, and the invoices from the supply companies..."

"And I know more tradesmen than we could ever need," said Desmond. "Plumbers, electricians, roofers, HVAC people..." He smiled, almost evilly. "Green Valley's going to regret not having me around anymore, especially since I'll be taking some of my old crews with me."

I stared back at the three of them, feeling a swell of happiness and pride. I was speechless. Or rather, virtually speechless.

"Holy shit."

The spreadsheet still glowed on the screen. It all made sense.

"I can do most of the carpentry myself," Desmond continued. "At least in the beginning. Not to mention Rogan's worked with me on a framing crew for three straight summers. Even Mason knows how to swing a hammer on weekends."

My pride was replaced by a sudden wave of panic. "You mean you're *all* quitting?"

"Not right away," Rogan admitted. "But eventually, yeah."

I was stunned. Astonished. A little frightened. But

also, so, so happy for them.

"So you're all leaving me," I chuckled, trying to make light of it.

"Well..." said Desmond. "Actually..."

He pushed a slip of paper forward, away from a group of others. They all had words on them. The one in front of me read: *Perfect Storm Construction.*

I scanned it three times, laughing each one. But the guys weren't laughing.

"It really is a perfect name," I said at last.

"It is..." agreed Mason. "But only if you're with us."

The words echoed again in my head, as the kitchen fell deathly silent. Each tick of the wall clock was now a thunderclap.

With us...

"We were going to go with *Fifth Wheel Builders,*" Desmond broke in. "But that had, well... sort of a negative connotation to it."

"Wait," I said. "W—With you?"

"Yes," said Rogan.

"As a partner?"

"Oh we definitely want you as a business partner," he explained. "But it's *so* much more than that..."

I tried to swallow, but my throat was bone dry. My heart was thumping a mile a minute, screaming away deep in my chest.

"We want you as our girlfriend, Alyssa," said Desmond, closing his hand over mine. "Totally. Completely."

"Officially," Rogan smiled, as he chimed in.

"You're *ours*," Mason murmured, adding a smile. "You have been for a while. And in case you haven't noticed... we *love* you."

The guys nodded solemnly as my eyes glassed over. I looked from Desmond, to Mason, to Rogan again. All three of them were staring back at me with the same deeply happy expression.

"I– I love you too!" I said, bursting into tears.

"Enough to be in business with us?" Desmond grinned.

"Enough to do *anything* with you!" I exclaimed, before I was enveloped in the mother of all four-way hugs.

Epilogue

ALYSSA

"You sure you're ready for this?"

I was stretched out over our new bed, across our all new sheets. In the master suite of our freshly rented, four-bedroom home.

"Ready as I'll ever be," I winked back at Desmond.

He smacked my naked ass hard enough to make me jump. I was sopping wet. So very ready...

"Let's go then," said Rogan impatiently, pulling me up and onto his hard body. "I can't wait another minute to get back inside you..."

I slid down on him, sighing as he filled me from within. Placing my hands on his perfect chest, I rolled my hips forward and back a few times as the others looked on.

"All set?" asked Mason, propped up alongside me.

I kissed him deeply, swirling my tongue through his mouth while still writhing against his friend. "Just enjoying the ride."

He laughed into my mouth, kissing me back with even

more passion than normal. And that's because tonight wasn't normal at all. Far from it.

Tonight we were celebrating.

Rogan's hands slid upward and kneaded my breasts. He dragged the pads of his thumbs over my most sensitive areas, urging me forward and back on his hardness.

Sixteen months...

That's how long it had been. The length of time since they'd first touched me, held me, made love to me — all at once. The way I loved it.

The way I loved *them*.

"Next time, I'm on the bottom," Mason murmured into my mouth.

"That's fine," I smiled, kissing him some more. I gave his incredible girth a firm, promising squeeze. "Especially since you're not fitting anywhere *else...*"

Sixteen months. Almost a year and a half together. Three houses built from scratch, and another four in the works. Two new plots of land in up-and-coming neighborhoods. One pending sale...

"God, you feel good," grunted Rogan from beneath me. His voice had that familiar tightness to it that I knew all too well. "Almost *too* good—"

"Don't you dare come yet," I sighed. Reluctantly I slowed down a little. I stopped grinding my ass every time I bottomed out, too. "If I'm sticking this out, *you're* sticking this out."

He laughed, blowing some of my hair out of his

mouth. It dangled down as I rode him, tickling his face as I looked pleadingly at Mason.

"I'm on it."

My third lover reached out and pinned the errant locks back behind my ears. Some of them, anyway.

Next time, ponytail.

I laughed at the absurdity of myself making mental notes. Still, there was a lot of logistics involved when it came to taking three guys at once. Especially considering what we were about to do.

I can't believe we're all finally together!

So much had happened over the last year, everything was still a whirlwind. Desmond's apartment had become home base for us. A place of business for one, but also the place we gathered, almost every night of the week.

It was three months after we started that Rogan moved in. Another six before Mason's lease ran out. I maintained my own apartment even longer, up until now. But moving into a house together was inevitable. It just made sense.

Besides, it saved us a shit-ton of money, too.

"Slide up a little more," Desmond murmured from behind me. "I'm about ready."

I felt Rogan shift, and a shiver of anticipation shot through me. I was about to do something *crazy*. Something I'd been working my way up to, and something we'd promised to try on the first night in our new place.

"Remember what we said," I smiled sweetly back at Desmond. "About going slow..."

"Yeah yeah," he said, stroking himself slowly up and down. His member was all slick and glistening. Totally covered in oil, as he inched behind me.

The cabin. It had all started there, and we'd gone back up this Christmas as well. With the business the way it was, we only took a few days this time. Hell, we didn't even ski.

But we screwed like crazy all over that place, remembering the blizzard that had brought us so close together.

That's not all you did there...

That part was true as well. Because it was over the past holiday, sandwiched gently between my three beautiful boyfriends, that I was introduced to anal for the very first time.

And who would've thought... I absolutely *loved* it.

It was so good in fact, that it pissed me off. I was angry at myself for having gone so long, and wasted every other year of my sex life without getting nailed in the ass.

Maybe it's because they were so good at it. Rogan and Desmond had been first and second, taking me slowly and carefully in that secret place no man ever had. I enjoyed it so much I even let Mason try... although I had to cut his little adventure short, almost halfway through.

'It was fun while it lasted,' he'd told me, with a rueful smile. I made sure to take extra good care of him for the rest of the trip, though. To make up for all that he was missing out on, while I let the others do me that way as much as their little hearts' desired.

And now here we were, on the first night in our new place; a house we all lived in together. A true family for the very first time. One day the four of us planned to design and construct our dream home. We'd build it from the ground up, and a whole new future along with it.

But that would come later. Because right now?

Right now I was about to get double-penetrated for the first time in *any* of our lives.

"Keep steady for a minute," said Desmond. "And don't move."

I felt his hands close over my hips. His fingers flexing to bring me closer, as Rogan slowed his thrusts to a stop, somewhere beneath me.

Either this is going to really *hurt...* I thought to myself. *Or it's going to be the best thing in the whole world.*

I was wise enough to realize it could go either way. But optimistic enough to hope for the latter.

Desmond spread my cheeks gently, and I braced for the inevitable. I felt the head pressed hotly against me, right up against my new favorite place.

"Do it."

He pushed in, as slow as could be. The lubrication did its job well. He slid inside, parting me perfectly. Filling my brain with that amazing sensation of being full, combined with the heated tingles of doing something naughty and forbidden.

"Oh... oh wow."

Desmond didn't 'wow' often. But when he did...

"This is tighter than I even imagined."

I held my ground, staring lovingly down at Rogan. Feeling the warmth of his chest pressed tightly against my breasts, as his friend filled my ass inch by wonderful inch.

"We good?" he asked, and kissed me.

"You tell me," I grinned.

"I can tell you I've never felt someone sliding into my girl while I was already *in* my girl," he admitted. "But damn if it isn't pretty damn hot."

Desmond's hands relaxed on my ass, and I knew he was almost in. He pushed some more, rocking us both forward, and then suddenly I felt the heat of his hard stomach pressed up against my backside.

"Congratulations," Mason chuckled. "You're a sexy sandwich."

Ohhhh....

My eyes dropped closed, my mind focusing on the exquisite new sensation of having *two* of my lovers inside me at the same time. It was unbelievably snug. Deliciously tight. But so totally, totally worth it...

"Go..." I nodded, dragging my hair across Rogan's chest. "Please. Take me."

They started one at a time, each of them testing our new limits. Slowly screwing me in and out, while the other held his position inside me.

Then they started going together... and my eyes rolled back into my head.

Fuuuuck.

It should've felt twice as good. Somehow though, it was way better than that.

MY GOD.

Nothing compared to the intensity! To the physical closeness of our three churning bodies, moving and writhing as one.

But there was an emotional edge too — a rush of excitement at being possessed by the both of them simultaneously. It was the best of both worlds. All the pleasure of having Rogan thrusting away, filling my wet, eager channel... magnified by the raw vulgarity of taking Desmond's thickness, buried so achingly deep in my ass.

"Oh my *God* that's good!"

Two gentle hands on my shoulders were holding me steady. Screwing me backwards on every thrust...

Mason.

I looked up into my third lover's gorgeous green eyes. They were already glazed over and gleaming with lust.

"C'mere baby," I breathed, reaching out for him. I smiled and licked my lips. "There's no *way* you're getting left out..."

It was the last piece of the puzzle. The missing link.

Yessss.

Mason rose before me, his incredible body rippling as he stood on the bed. I closed my fingers around his thick baton... and somehow got my mouth over it.

Mmmmmm...

And just like that we were all connected — everyone at once. Time and again, I'd told the guys that all I wanted was to be the center of their world.

And now here I was.

What's next, Alyssa?

A thousand things. Ten thousand adventures. Building and selling. Buying... and then building again.

Yes, but what's next for all of you?

We'd discussed the future, and it only got brighter. Love. Life. Laughter. The building of a home. Settling down, and then filling that home with children...

All three of my men wanted families. And big ones at that.

Could you do it?

Oh God, I sure could. I'd thought so much lately about bringing life into the world. And then the best part of all — sharing that life with the three men I loved more than anything, and who always loved me.

Children.

I couldn't wait to carry their babies. I'd told all three of them, almost right from the start. Everything we'd done together had been unorthodox at best. But if my life were unorthodox, yet deliriously happy?

Well... I could live with that.

"I'm going to come..." said a voice, somewhere far away. My eyes fluttered open. It could've been anyone.

"When you do..." I gasped. "Make sure you come together..."

Rogan let out a grunt-fueled laugh. "What are we, magicians?"

I squeezed down on him in punishment, enhancing his torment.

"Okay okay..." he breathed. "Just... let me know... when—"

"NOW."

Desmond exploded with that single word, going off like a volcano. Spilling his molten seed high in my ass.

"That's it," I gasped. "Squeeze it..."

His hands flexed, his fingers digging into my flesh. It all felt good. It felt right.

"Squeeze my ass as you come inside me..."

His palms opened and closed, twisting my ass hard in his hands. Sending mixed signals of euphoria and pain, all the way up my spine, to the pleasure centers of my brain.

"GOD yes!"

I cried out at the penultimate moment, then climaxed all over *both* of their thrusting shafts. I felt like a collapsing star, finally going supernova. Releasing every last ounce of love and heat and energy all at once, expending it in a brilliant eruption of bliss and contentment.

When I looked down, Rogan's face was already contorted with exuberance. He'd let go without me even realizing it, filling me to overflowing. Spending every last drop of himself inside my body, as the three of us struggled to fill our lungs with sweet, delicious oxygen.

Mason!

I rolled away from them, into the center of the bed. Stretching my arms out in Mason's direction, while spreading my thighs obscenely wide for him.

"Take me..."

He didn't have to be asked twice. He slipped between my legs and slid straight inside.

"I mean really *take* me."

Our mouths met so forcefully our teeth clacked, and then he was kissing me like I'd never been kissed. I clawed his back. Thrust my tongue deep into his sweet mouth, as Mason pounded me again and again, driving me deep into the center of our new bed.

OHHHHH...

His ass moved like a machine! My hands slid downward, to marvel at the musculature just beneath his skin. To feel his glutes flexing and unflexing, as he pumped me so hard I thought he might break me in half.

He's so deep!

It felt like being drilled. Being cored out, by some kind of otherworldly—

Holy shit Alyssa, it's so deep it's—

I clawed at Mason's ass, my freshly-manicured fingernails digging in. He grunted like an animal, as his jaw went suddenly tight.

Oh thank GOD.

Our mouths parted. Our eyes locked. Mason looked straight at me — straight past me without even seeing me — and then his mouth opened in a perfect 'O', and I knew what came next.

"Yes, baby!"

The first pulse felt like a *cannon*. Firing into me. Destroying me from the inside out.

"*YESSSS...*"

My second orgasm was a lot like my first, only more concentrated, more focused. I wrapped my legs around him as best I could, desperately trying to keep him in. Not that it mattered. He wasn't stopping until he was finished.

"I... I think..."

I smiled at him through the unadulterated pleasure. Through the haze of distant numbness and pain, outweighed by the ecstasy of—

"I think I found the bottom of your pussy."

I nodded and laughed and pressed my lips to his, my face all sweaty, my hair getting between our mouths as we kissed.

"I'm pretty sure you did."

God it felt like all new territory! But the discomfort was dull and distant. And the pleasure was oh so ridiculously *good*.

"I'm going to feel that tomorrow," I nodded dreamily. I hooked my thigh around him and pulled him against me. "And maybe the day after, too..."

I knew beyond a shadow of a doubt I was right. The ache was there already, faint and deep and wonderful.

"Way to break in the new bed," Rogan chided, throwing us a pair of clean towels.

"Not to mention the new place," I added.

In the next room, the big glass shower kicked on. I could hear Desmond already stepping into it.

"Should we break that in also?"

Rogan looked at Mason, then shook his head. "Can you believe this insatiable bitch?"

"Hey, I'm just talking about showering," I purred playfully, stretching my arms overhead. "As for anything else... I'm probably gonna need a minute."

"You're gonna need more than a minute," Mason joked.

"Yeah," I laughed, elbowing him as he got up from the bed. I smirked over my shoulder at Rogan. "He *broke* me."

Sixteen months. That's all it was. A year and a half, and everything had changed.

"You coming while the water's still hot?"

I broke from my trance of watching them; two rounded, well-muscled asses walking away. One of them now riddled with nail-marks.

Three men.

My men.

"You greedy, insatiable bitch," I laughed to no one in particular.

And the ceiling stared back at me in silence.

Need *more* Reverse Harem?

Thanks for checking out *The Christmas Toy - A Holiday Reverse Harem Romance* . Here's hoping you totally LOVED it!

And for even *more* sweltering reverse harem heat? Check out: *Saving Savannah - A Reverse Harem Romance*. Below you'll find a preview of the sexy, sizzling cover, plus the first several chapters so you can see for yourself:

The Christmas Toy - Krista Wolf

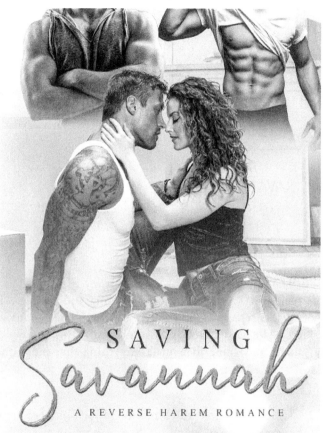

Chapter One

SAVANNAH

"You can just put that anywhere..."

The mover bent at the knees, but my eyes stayed glued to his bare arms. His great biceps, bulging and flexing. The cut of his triceps, straining against those broad, muscular shoulders. He was covered in a thin sheen of sweat now. An extra glisten and shine that made everything that much more delicious.

"Ma'am?"

I shook my head to clear it of my self-induced trance. The other two men were standing there waiting on me, holding another pair of the heavier boxes.

"Okay those..." I pointed one by one. "Living room. Bedroom." Then, adding my sweetest smile: "Please."

They shuffled off in opposite directions, leaving my eyes torn with a hard decision. Each of them had an amazingly firm, rounded ass. Ultimately I went with the blond, whose jeans were tighter.

"You should start unpacking," the first man said with a chuckle. "Looks like you've got your work cut out for you."

"I'd still rather help," I said, following him down the stairs.

"You really don't have to," he replied. "That's what you hired us for."

"I know. But still..."

The number I'd called on the flyer said something about 'College Hunks'. It came complete with the graphic of a handsome, barrel-chested youth with big, strong arms.

I just never imagined I'd actually *get* someone like that.

Much less three someones.

And yet here they were — almost exactly like the little caricature on the flyer. Three giant, college-age movers with bulging arms and square-set jaws. They met me at the truck, down in the street. Each looking more chiseled and beautiful than the one before.

"You've got an *awful* lot of stuff," the first one said as we reached the truck. He stood on the sidewalk for a second, setting his strong hands on his slender hips. "It's just you up there?"

I hesitated for an awkward moment. Eventually, I nodded.

"Sorry ma'am," he said immediately. "I didn't mean to pry."

"No, it's alright."

"It isn't, really," he replied. "I shouldn't be—"

"Calling me ma'am?" I chuckled. "The others look like they're in college, but you..."

He turned to look back at me, and his blue eyes sparkled. "Twenty-six."

"Ah, now see? You're a few years older than me!"

A smile curled its way up one side of his mouth, splitting his gorgeous, stubbled face. God, he was beautiful. So strong and savage-looking.

"Tell ya what," I said, returning his grin. "Start calling me Savannah, and I'll start calling you..."

"Erik," he said, wiping one palm on his jeans. "With a K."

He extended his hand, which was attached to a very tattooed arm. I shook it, noticing how big and calloused and amazing it was.

"Nice to meet you, Erik with a K."

"Likewise."

His touch lingered on mine for just an extra half second. Then he nodded and hopped back up into the truck.

"The Italian Stallion back there is Roman by the way," Erik called from the top of the ramp. "And the blond one's Zane."

"Ah," I acknowledged. "Either of them actually in college?"

"Roman is," he replied with a grin. "The rest of us are just hunks."

With a grunt, he lifted the next box and carried it down the ramp. I stacked two of the smaller ones against my chest and followed.

My God, his ass is fantastic...

It was a little salacious maybe, perving out like this. But for the past hour I'd been really enjoying the view. And hey, if I were being honest — it had been a while. Much longer than I actually liked to admit.

We made our way back to my new apartment, which amazed me every time I walked through the door. A big wide studio, with smooth oak floors and beautifully molded walls, it was easily double the size of any place I'd ever lived before.

I almost wanted to pinch myself again, to make sure I wasn't dreaming.

"How many more?" asked Zane, the blond one. Like the others, he'd stripped off his brightly-colored uniform, and was down to a sleeveless white T-shirt that hugged his lithe, beautiful body. I could even see the hint of his sculpted abdominals, straining against the fabric as he caught his breath.

"More than enough," Erik chuckled. "It's like the truck keeps refilling itself." His eyes darted playfully to me. "I think she's moving three whole families in here."

"Five," I countered, without missing a beat.

"See?" said Erik, with a laugh. "I told ya she's one of us."

Just then the Italian Stallion stomped in from the back bedroom. He was tall and dark and devilishly handsome, a little fact that certainly hadn't escaped my notice.

"Roman, Zane," said Erik with a gesture. "This here is Savannah, not 'ma'am'."

I smiled pleasantly and nodded.

"Savannah, these are my chucklehead friends."

I reached out to shake each of their hands, then turned back to Erik. "Are *all* of your friends chuckleheads?"

"Only the best ones."

"I see."

Introductions finished, we headed back down for the rest of my stuff. It took the better part of another two hours, even with four of us, before we were staring at the back wall of the moving truck. Box by box, step by step, the last of my things was finally carried up three flights of overly-steep stairs. It left us breathless and heaving, leaning against the barren walls.

"Damn," said Roman. He made his way through the kitchen and started filling a plastic cup with tap water. "That was a rough one."

I watched him drink, the water moving in rhythmic gulps down his magnificent throat. He had the jawline of a boxer. The hands of one, too.

"At least you didn't have any couches," chuckled Zane. "Or loungers. Or..." He paused and scratched his head. "Hey, where *is* all your furniture anyway?"

"In those boxes," I smiled, pointing.

His innocent eyes went wide. "Seriously?"

"Yup. Everything's all brand new." I raised my shoulders in a little shrug. "Figured I'd give myself a fresh start."

Roman mopped the back of his sun-bronzed neck with the bandana that had been hanging out of his front pocket all day. "Well it doesn't get much fresher than this."

Zane walked the room in a circle, admiring the high ceilings. "You're going to be here all week putting this stuff together," he said, gesturing around.

"Probably," I agreed.

"Oh definitely," said Erik. He plucked a large bottle of wine from the kitchen counter. "At least you have this, though. You were thinking ahead."

"Actually," I admitted, "that was left here for me. A little gift, from the previous tenants."

Erik lifted the tiny card next to the bottle read it. "Wow," he said. "You mean there are still nice people left in this world?"

"A few," I laughed. "Probably not many."

"That's an *awful* lot of wine," Zane noted, scratching at his shaggy blond mane.

"Yeah," I chuckled. "Too bad you guys won't be here later to help me finish it."

The words were fun, flirty. They'd just slipped out. But the way the guys were suddenly eyeing each other, it made my stomach erupt in butterflies.

"I think you're just angling for someone to put your furniture together," Erik insinuated with a wry grin.

"That too."

He looked again at the others, then raised an eyebrow. "Would there be pizza involved?"

My heart was pounding now, hammering a steady rhythm in my chest. "Could be, yeah."

The guys looked at each other again. All three of them gave up a mutual shrug.

"Then we're in," said Zane.

Roman folded his arms and nodded.

"Let's say eight o'clock?" suggested Erik. "Gives us time to run home and shower. Come back without the stupid uniforms."

"And what if I *like* you in the stupid uniforms?" I flirted, for no particular reason.

Erik's smoldering blue eyes bored into mine. I knew right then I was in trouble. *Big* trouble.

"Trust me," he winked. "You'll like us better without em'."

Two

SAVANNAH

It took them just ten minutes to put my kitchen table together, and another twenty to assemble the chairs. I'd bought a cheap set. Nothing fancy. But it seemed more than adequate, as the four of us sat huddled around it in my brightly-lit kitchen.

"Wanna pass me the salt, bro?"

Zane slid it across the table, toward his friend's waiting hand. He went too hard though. Halfway there, it tipped on its side and spilled out in a cool-looking fan pattern.

"C'mon man," said Erik. "Have some respect. She hasn't even set up yet and you're wrecking the place already."

Zane righted the shaker apologetically and began the cleanup process. Before he did though, Roman took a pinch of the spilled salt and tossed it over his opposite shoulder.

"What's that for?" asked Zane.

"Good luck," I answered for him.

Roman turned his attention my way and gave me a very approving look. "So... you're Italian?"

I pulled at my deep red curls and laughed. "Do I *look* Italian?"

I was leaning back in my chair a bit, balancing precariously. The pizza was great. So was the company. Two glasses of wine in, I was feeling no pain.

"No," Roman finally admitted.

"Call me superstitious then," I said with a shrug. "I just happen to know a lot of that stupid 'old wives tales' stuff."

"It's not stupid if it works," he replied smoothly.

Zane laughed and twisted the cap off another beer from the six pack he'd been sharing with Erik. "And how would you even know if it works?" he asked Roman. "Have you been having especially good luck lately?"

Roman's soft brown eyes found mine. His smile was charming as he tipped his glass in my direction. "Can't really complain so far."

We were a couple of hours into our move-in party, which included the assembly of five pieces of furniture so far. The end tables in the living room were done, the entertainment center, all screwed together. The couch would arrive tomorrow, the television the day after that. As for my bed...

Well, the guys had set the box-spring on its brand new frame, and enjoyed peeling the protective plastic off my brand new mattress. When they saw it was a King, they made jokes about my boyfriend or husband showing up at any minute. In reality though, I'd picked it because the room was just *really* big. That, plus I loved to stretch out.

We'd unpacked the kitchen together, and the bathroom also. Everything of course, was brand new. From the still-in-the-box coffee-maker to the bright red price tags slapped on the bottom of my dishes.

"You really *are* getting a fresh start," whistled Zane. He looked me up and down and squinted. "You come up here from Georgia?"

"Why?" I teased, adding an exaggerated twang to my not-so-southern drawl. "Just because my name's *Sav-ann-ah?*"

His mouth opened and then closed, causing me to laugh and tip my wine back against my lips. I was enjoying how red he was turning, beneath his lion-blond mane.

"Well you're sure not from Massachusetts," Zane continued to blush. "Much less from *Salem.*"

Salem. It had been the place I'd finally settled on. Not so much at random, but for purposes I hoped would ultimately pan out for me. And if for some reason they didn't...

If they didn't, you know exactly what to do.

I shook the intrusive thoughts away. Salem was every bit as perfect as I imagined it would be. Small. Sleepy. Charming in its sense of rich history, but also just crowded enough to blend in and not really be noticed.

Especially around this time of year.

"Well I think we're about finished for the night," I said, tracing the rim of my glass with one finger.

Disappointment fell over their faces like a curtain of gloom. I had to stifle a smile.

"It *is* getting late," Erik agreed, draining his beer. "I guess we'll pack our tools and head out."

"Oh I didn't say *that*," I corrected him. "I just meant we're done putting stuff together. I'm tired of hammering and screwing things. And you guys have done more than enough work for me today."

Hope dawned for them again, bright and clear. This time I actually chuckled. I'd forgotten how much fun it was, flirting like this.

"I don't have a television," I shrugged. "Or a radio. Or even a couch. But I do have *something* to make us a little more comfortable."

Roman grinned. Erik rubbed at his jaw with one tattooed hand.

"Oh yeah?" Zane asked carefully. "And what's that?"

I got up, stretched my tired legs, and crossed into the empty expanse of the living room.

"Come and see."

Three

SAVANNAH

"Okay then..." I purred, squirming my ass into the pillow. I took an emboldening sip of wine. Leaning back a little bit, the softness felt good beneath me. "Your turn."

Zane grinned, pretending to stroke his chin thoughtfully. But he already had it. He already knew.

"Never have I ever... had sex in public."

We were sitting in a circle, cross-legged, facing each other as we played the game. The only thing keeping our asses from the hard wooden floor were a series of fluffy red throw pillows I'd bought on a whim, that I hoped would match the couch when it finally showed up.

Erik and Zane both drank, indicating they'd done the deed. As they tipped their beers back in surrender I drank as well, straight from the quickly-dwindling bottle of wine.

"Here," smiled Roman, reaching in my direction.

"Might as well make it unanimous."

Our hands touched, his fingers lingering on mine for a few seconds as our eyes met. He drank deeply from the bottle we were sharing, but without breaking our gaze.

"Alright," I said. "Out with it."

"Stories?" asked Zane hopefully.

"Of course."

The pillows had been my idea, but the game of course had come from the guys. It had taken all of two rounds before it got sexual. And that was only because they were being polite.

I didn't mind at all. It was kinda fun.

"It was on a pool table," Erik began, "in the back room of a shitty bar. Pool tables are *hard*, by the way. I don't recommend them."

We laughed as he pretended to rub at his sore lower back. Zane went on to detail having sex in the ocean, submerged up to his neck at a semi-crowded beach. Roman's public romp was more adventurous, having taken place in the changing room of a department store.

"Your girl must've been trying on lingerie," I quipped, still looking into those chocolate brown eyes.

"Who said there was a girl involved?" joked Zane, making an obscene back and forth hand motion. We all broke out laughing, even Roman.

"I don't even remember what she was trying on," he eventually smiled, staring back at me. "But now you."

I took a deep breath, then relayed my own little story about screwing an ex-boyfriend standing up, while jammed between two parked cars. The guys hung on my every word. Their faces were priceless.

"In broad daylight?" Erik smirked.

"It was dark-*ish*..." I said, holding my hand out sideways. "Hey, what can I say," I shrugged. "We hadn't seen each other in a long time."

"You could've gone *inside* the car," Zane pointed out.

"You ever try screwing in the back of a tiny car?" I asked boldly. When the guys all laughed, I nodded. "Exactly."

The turn passed to Roman, so all eyes fell on him. As he looked to the ceiling trying to come up with something good, the voice in the back of my mind started in again.

Ummm... what the hell are you doing?

God, who knew the voice of reason could be so annoying! And sing-songy. And annoying. Did I mention annoying?

Playing Never Have I Ever, I answered glibly. *On the floor of my living room. With the three hot moving hunks I've been hanging out with all day. That's what.*

The voice didn't have an answer. For a moment or two, at least.

But should you really—

I shoved the voice back again, tucking it away before it could convince me otherwise. I was enjoying myself. Having a great time with these guys, on the first night in my new apartment. In truth, I craved the company. The alternative was a lonely, eerily quiet night in this big empty place. No television, no music. Nothing but my phone to keep me company, and that was no company at all.

"Never have I ever... slept with a total stranger," said Roman, drinking almost immediately afterward. The others drank too, as he held the bottle out to me with a fiendish smile.

"Hang on a second," I said, waving the bottle away. "Define 'total stranger'."

He hesitated for a moment, his gorgeous bronze face going abruptly thoughtful. "Someone you knew less than half a day."

My lips came together wryly. I reached for the bottle, as the others broke out in laughter.

"Yeah," Roman chuckled. "Thought so."

I took my time, watching them as I drank. Enjoying the warmth of their camaraderie, the feeling of closeness and friendship between them. It was obvious, the bonds they shared. They were a lot more than just coworkers.

The strength of their connection made me a little jealous.

"Alright gorgeous," Erik winked at me. "Your turn."

I'd had something before, but now it seemed a little too tame. We'd gone into more interesting territory. I didn't want to backtrack.

"Hmm..." I said, stalling for something good. "Let me think."

God, they were all so fucking *hot*. They'd shown up clean and showered and shaved, except Erik, who'd kept his stubble. They were still in tight jeans, though. Shirts that seemed form-fitted to their strong, muscular bodies. I wondered absently how much of that muscle came from carrying heaving things up and down staircases. The rest *had* to have come from the gym.

"Never have I ever... gotten head while driving," I blurted daringly. The guys stared back at me, pleasantly shocked. I felt my pulse kick up a few notches as I added: "Or *given* it."

"Now *there's* a fucking turn!" laughed Roman, pointing my way. He reached out for the bottle, but I drank deeply first, before handing it back to him.

"Wow," Erik whistled. "Really?"

"Uh huh," I said coyly. "Surprised?"

His expression could best be described as shocked admiration. "Guess not."

I looked back at them in our little circle, feeling flush with heat. Not just from the wine, but from the observation that every one of us had inched significantly closer since the game had started.

"You're *all* drinking," I noticed, watching their bottles go up with a chuckle. "So do all guys get head while driving?"

"Oh yeah," said Zane immediately.

Erik nodded his agreement. "Common sexual bucket-lister."

I laughed again, my eyes lingering on his broad, beautiful shoulders. He leaned back on both arms, causing his massive triceps to flex outward against that smooth, perfect skin.

"Alright, this round's Truth or Dare again," Roman announced from my left. He looked directly at me. "So... Truth or Dare?"

"Truth."

All three of them went silent for a long moment. It was the first 'truth' turn I'd taken since the game began. But I was ready for anything.

Almost anything.

"Are you really from Georgia?" he finally asked.

The smile left my face all at once. I couldn't help it.

"Forget it," I said quickly. "I'll take the Dare then."

"No no," Zane said, wagging his finger. "You already said tru—"

"Hey, let the girl do a dare if she wants to," Erik cut in. He shot me a quick look. "It might be a lot more interesting."

Relief flooded through me as I returned his grin with a grateful smile. He nodded back.

"Alright then," Roman said matter-of-factly. He looked me up and down, those penetrating brown eyes straying strategically and unapologetically over my body. I knew something bigger was coming. The warmth spreading in my belly told me well in advance.

"I dare you to kiss me."

Four

SAVANNAH

Butterflies. Schoolgirl butterflies. They fluttered against my insides, sending electric shivers from the nape of my neck to the base of my spine.

Even so, I didn't hesitate.

In for a penny...

I leaned forward and pressed my lips against Roman's full, beautiful mouth. He was kissing me back in an instant. Cradling the side of my face in one strong, gentle hand, while his mouth churned and his jaw rotated against mine.

In for a...

I gasped as his hand sifted its way into my hair. His tongue slipped past my lips, probing against mine, and my whole body came alive with fireworks.

Holy shit.

It felt absolutely incredible! Like a billion nerve

endings exploding all at once, sending waves of pleasure rippling through my brain. My eyes closed, as my hands wandered his thick, corded arms. I could feel the muscles there, coiled just beneath his warm, mocha-colored skin.

This... This is probably...

I didn't know what it was. I only knew I wanted *more* of it. That I wanted to keep on kissing him, over and over again. I wanted him to keep holding me, to pull me tightly against his chest with those big, beautiful arms...

"A—Ahem!"

The sound of someone clearing their throat jolted us back to reality. I settled backward, returning to my pillow. My mouth remained half open, my lips still swollen and wet from having practically just made out with this gorgeous, dark-haired stranger.

Practically?

"Wow," I heard Erik say. "Holy... just *wow.*"

"My turn," said Zane immediately. I was still reeling, though. Still flushed with embarrassment and excitement and —

"I dare you to kiss *me,* also."

My heart was pounding. The butterflies in my stomach had been replaced by a roller-coaster, as I snorted theatrically. "Yeah, right."

One look in his sky-blue eyes told me he wasn't kidding. The others dropped back a bit, leaving the two of us just staring at each other. Zane leaned forward on two long arms. As our faces drew nearer, I realized I was already falling forward myself.

What in the world—

Our lips met, and I was kissing him too. Not just kissing but *exploring* him, running my hands over his shoulders as he took me into his arms.

This isn't just kissing.

It was and it wasn't. We were certainly kissing — there was no mistake about that. But our hands began roaming like they had minds of their own. I could feel a warm palm sliding down my back. It pierced the waistband of my jeans, stopping only to cup one globe of my smooth, bare ass.

"It's a G-string," I murmured into Zane's beautiful mouth, as I felt him feeling around. "Don't get excited or anything."

I couldn't believe how bold he was... until I took stock of my own situation. I had one arm draped over his shoulder, twirling at the long blond hair at the back of his head. The other was busy tracing itself over his lithe, wonderful chest. Feeling the hard edges of his two big pectorals, before turning palm-side down as I slid even lower, to test every ridge and ripple of his hard, six-pack abdominals beneath my fingertips.

Whoa...

By this time I'd practically climbed into his lap. We were kissing like we were the only two people in the room, which of course we weren't. That part should've made me feel nervous, or uncomfortable, or weird.

To my surprise however, it was having the opposite effect.

You love *this.*

I really did. Even more than that though, I *needed* it. The contact. The closeness. The sensation of someone else's hands settling over my hips. The all-too long ago warmth and feel of actual human touch.

Another set of hands slid over me, guiding me to one side. I turned my head and suddenly I was kissing Erik, deeply, passionately. Rubbing one delicate hand against the sandpaper surface of his roughly stubbled face, as my tongue slid eagerly into his mouth, seeking to find his own.

This is crazy. This is nuts.

Erik's mouth tasted sweet, like strawberries and beer. I drank him in. I grabbed his head as Zane bounced me gently into his lap, grinding upward from beneath until I could feel a distinct bulge forming in the crotch of his jeans.

"Truth or Dare..." a voice whispered hotly into my ear.

"Dare," I shivered.

I was still making out with Erik when a pair of lips began planting kisses along the line of my exposed throat. Vaguely I recognized Roman, nuzzling into me. Dragging his hot mouth tantalizingly across my bare skin.

"I dare you to take us in *there*," he murmured, nodding over my shoulder, "and break in your new bed with us."

Two hands had found their way up my shirt. They cupped my breasts, kneading them gently. Making my areolae instantly hard.

"I... I..."

I didn't have the words. Couldn't think of a single reason why I shouldn't take them up on their offer. Moreover, I didn't have the resolve.

Not that I wanted it, mind you.

My eyes flared open hungrily, betraying my lust. I was way too far gone. My palms slipped beneath my own shirt and captured Roman's, as I slid my hands over his.

"Never have I ever been with more than one person at a time..." I murmured, looking right into his eyes.

A second later I found myself being lifted against a hard chest. Held easily by two strong, granite-like arms.

"We can fix that," he said, as he carried me out of the room.

Five

SAVANNAH

I was all in. Ready for anything as I was carried into my shadowy bedroom, and spread out across the fresh-from-the-package new sheets. They were taking turns kissing me. Taking turns *undressing* me. My whole world was a flurry of lips and hands and fingertips, dragging themselves over my body.

And I was loving every second of it.

It's not like you haven't actually thought about this.

I had, of course. For as long as I could remember, I'd had fantasies of being with more than one guy. Deep, dark fantasies of being shared and traded and passed around. Of splitting my attention between two or more men, and being pampered and worshiped by them as well.

And yet, I'd never come close. I'd never encountered guys who felt comfortable doing such things around each other, and it seemed I was the master of picking the most jealous boyfriends on the planet.

But now here I was, lying in my own bed. Kissing the most beautiful blond creature I'd ever laid eyes on, while the gorgeous brown-eyed Italian on the other side of me closed his mouth over one warm, welcoming breast.

And then there was Erik, between my legs. He'd pulled off my jeans, and now he was nuzzling his way up the insides of my bare, quivering thighs.

Ohhhhh...

Every kiss was electric. Every touch of his lips made me jump and shiver. I felt his fingertips play softly over my mound, rubbing up and down a few times before pulling my G-string gently aside.

Oh my God.

Then he buried his face in my already-drenched crease, and the rest of the world came screeching to a halt.

Holy FUCK.

Slowly, sensually, he dragged his tongue along the most sensitive areas on the outside of my glistening slit. I shivered and bucked, holding Roman's head tightly against my chest. Kissing Zane wildly, as if somehow the three of them were in tune with one another.

"MMMMmmmm..."

I moaned into Zane's beautiful mouth as a finger slid inside me. One finger became two, gliding in and out, pumping me slow and deep.

I sucked in my next breath as a shuddering gasp. Trying to determine if I might be dreaming, or if this whole thing were actually real.

They're just. Too. Perfect.

Erik's hand was working true magic between my legs. His thumb fluttered over my button, as his mouth continued kissing and licking and sucking gently on my most sensitive areas. Somehow my fingers wound their way into his hair. I rolled my knuckles tight and bucked upward, showing him his affections were more than appreciated.

Are you seriously doing this?

In my mind it was already done. There was no reason in the world I shouldn't screw the living daylights out of the three hot moving guys I'd been flirting with for most of the day. There was absolutely no downside to just letting myself go, and marking the first night in my new apartment as an experience I'd always remember.

But you don't even know them!

That part was naughty... maybe even a bit dirty, too. But it was also the part that was most appealing to me. Not knowing them made it somehow okay, and giving myself over became that much easier. Besides, after tonight there was a good chance I wouldn't see any of them again. Strangely, it took the pressure off.

Besides, in my own weird way I trusted them. They'd been funny and fun. Incredibly sweet instead of crude, and totally laid back instead of pushy. The three of them had been just as ready to kiss me on the cheek and say goodbye as they had been to carry me into the bedroom. To me, that actually meant something.

And right now, it was all so natural. The way they moved, almost as one. The camaraderie and chemistry between us. Each of them had fallen instantly into an individual role, while pleasuring me at the same time. Almost like they'd done this before...

Had they?

Right now I didn't care. Erik's churning, swirling mouth had me at the very edge of nirvana, a feeling made even more intense by his long, talented fingers. Up top, the other two men had traded places. Roman was making out with me so slowly and sensually it was like he was the god of kissing. And Zane had his face buried between my breasts, giving them both ample attention. Tracing circles along my stiffening areola with the tip of his hot, pink tongue.

I felt the bed shift, and my thighs spread even wider. Erik was kneeling between my legs now, as the others stopped what they were doing to watch. He pushed the head of a fantastic-looking cock against my eager entrance, before pausing to look down at me.

"You okay with this?" he murmured softly.

I bit my lip and nodded, trying to be coy. Trying not to look as horny and desperate and ready as I actually was.

Erik lowered his hard body against mine, his incredible tattooed arms going to either side of my head. I sighed softly, as his lips hovered just above my own.

"Because unless you say otherwise," he growled throatily, "I'm going to *fuck* you."

I grunted back at him and bucked my hips in response.

"You'd better."

SAVING SAVANNAH IS NOW ON AMAZON!

Grab it now – It's free to read on Kindle Unlimited!

ABOUT THE AUTHOR

Krista Wolf is a lover of action, fantasy and all good horror movies... as well as a hopeless romantic with an insatiably steamy, dirtier side.

She writes suspenseful, mystery-infused stories filled with blistering hot twists and turns. Tales in which headstrong, impetuous heroines are the irresistible force thrown against the immovable object of powerful, alpha heroes.

If you like intelligent and witty romance served up with a panty-dropping, erotic edge? You've just found your new favorite author.

Click here to see all titles on

[Krista's Author Page](#)

Sign up to Krista's VIP Email list to get instant notification of all new releases: http://eepurl.com/dkWHab

Printed in Great Britain
by Amazon